Sentinel Rising

Andrea Drew

"Oh, what a tangled web we weave when first we practise to deceive."   Walter Scott

CONTENTS

Acknowledgments   i

Chapter 1   Pg 1

Chapter 2   Pg 19

Chapter 3   Pg 40

Chapter 4   Pg 61

Chapter 5   Pg 80

Chapter 6   Pg 88

Chapter 7   Pg 105

Chapter 8   Pg 130

Chapter 9   Pg 147

Chapter 10   Pg 170

Epilogue   Pg 188

ACKNOWLEDGMENTS

Thank you to my editor Rainy Kaye for taking my wrangled ramblings and straightening them out.

CHAPTER 1

Valentine's Day

He hadn't meant to kill the love of his life. As he stared at the lifeless form, a mess of tangled limbs on the soft carpet, a chill seeped up his spine, through his veins, and deep into the marrow of his bones.

He missed her so much, his darling Lauren. The love of his life, mother to his only child. How could she betray him? After all they'd been through, how could their life together be forgotten and dismissed as if none of it had ever happened? The secret conversations, the gossip, the problems solved together, the whispered moments before they drifted off to sleep—none of it mattered anymore. The loving Lauren he'd known had been caring and affectionate. Not the cold unfeeling bitch from hell that had screeched like an animal, told him he had no say in her life or in their child's life. When had she become uninterested in what he had to say?

When he had tried to explain why they should stay together, her eyes had glazed over and shifted to her computer, to a picture on the wall, to the clothes he was wearing, but never to his face, never to meet his gaze.

Her bright blue eyes had no longer reflected anything. She'd moved on a long time ago and taken her soul with her. He hadn't realised how screwed up and selfish she had become until their final confrontation.

He hadn't meant to kill her, but now she lay still next to the filing cabinet where she had hit her head. She was gone forever and never coming back. At first, he'd tried to wake her up. He'd told her he was sorry, and that he never should have yelled at her like that or pushed her. When she hadn't responded, he'd gone into panic mode, wrapping her in a sheet he'd pulled from the bed. But then he'd had no idea what to do with her body. He had knelt beside her, brushing her hair and removing the smeared makeup from under her unseeing eyes. Then the rush of what he'd done strangled him, closing his throat and filling him as he bellowed her name.

The immediacy of the moment, the reality of it hurt, ears ringing and the reverberations in the room pushing back at him. The loss of all he held dear, everything that truly mattered to him had been taken as if it never existed. He should have controlled himself better, and positively should never have pushed her so hard she fell backwards and hit her head on the corner of the cabinet. A fierce dark beast had possessed him, burned its way inside his ribcage somehow, demanding to be heard, to be avenged, to win.

Now he'd lost, really lost. There would be no

coming back from this. The emptiness wouldn't leave, his chest a brittle shell of nothingness, like the dead animals he saw by the side of the road before they'd been splattered to a pulp, their fur matted and blowing in the back wind from each passing car. He almost wanted the searing pain back, the fury, something to reassure him he still retained some essence that made him human.

He pulled the sheet over her face and lifted her in his arms. She was heavy. He held her there, swaying for a few seconds, suffering under the weight, wishing for more pain to ease his guilt, penance for a crime that could never be repaid.

The clock beside the bed said 11.49pm. It was Sunday night, so few people would be on the roads. The neighbours pretty much kept to themselves, and no lights from the local industrial estate were twinkling in the distance. No one would see them.

He carried her out to his car, pressed the automatic unlocking device on his keys, and laid her carefully in the boot. He wished he had a pillow to put underneath her head, but she'd be safe for now.

He opened the passenger door and climbed in, and then started up the ignition. They had both loved it out here, and sometimes they'd sit at their favourite look out spot on the cliff, gazing out to the coast, surrounded by the city lights below them. There were still some reminders of civilization but not enough to distract them. He would take her there now. She would be happy with Wilson's Point as her final resting place.

Sweat prickled up his arms. He pushed down on the button to his right and the pane of glass from the driver's side window disappeared with a whir. Memories pushed their way in: their first meeting, the first time they made love, and the first time they'd planned a future as they lay in bed, their feet intertwined.

He didn't know how long he drove, but eventually he recognised the turnoff for their special spot. As he stepped out of the car, the bright moon watched over him, lighting the area for the task ahead. It had to be done quickly. Opening the back of the car, he reached over for the shovel, and walked eight steps to a low hanging tree. Testing the ground for softness, he found the perfect place for Lauren to rest a couple of metres away where tree roots weren't poking through the earth.

He began to dig, tentatively initially. Then he thought about Lauren waiting in the back of the car, sleeping inside her pink sheet. He dug harder, the hole small at first, and then he lengthened it until there was enough room for her to rest in. Droplets of sweat formed on his spine, and then gathered into a trickle. He put down the shovel and returned to the car. Placing one arm under the back of her knees and the other just under her shoulders, he heaved her into his arms. At five foot four, she'd never been a big woman and, at that moment, he was thankful for her slender figure.

He trudged over to the hole and squatted down to lay her in it.

"Goodbye, darling. I'm so sorry," he whispered. "Forgive me, please. I'll never forget you."

He began shoveling dirt from the pile beside the hole to cover her. Once done, he patted the area down as best he could, brushed the dirt off his hands, and got back into the car for the return trip to Melbourne.

It had been so long since Connor Reardon got a late-night call—more than two years, in fact. In a previous life, he'd accepted the calls at ungodly hours as par for the course. It was always one dispatcher or another, telling him in a bored tone there had been another murder and he needed to get his butt to the crime scene. Eventually he'd quit in disgust, tired of the red tape and politics from the brass.

When he'd initially awoke, jolted from sleep by the sudden noise, he'd been in the middle of a bizarre vision, one in which his brother was still alive, and his nephew hadn't been incarcerated for killing a detective.

Fat chance.

He opened his eyes and let them adjust to the dim light from the window. The still form of his fiancé, Gypsy Shields lay to his right. It would take more than a ringing telephone to wake her. His phone continued to buzz its way across the dark laminated top of his bedside table. He dragged his left arm from beneath the covers to find the lamp. The phone screen cast a glow, and he sat up in bed. Finding the lamp, he flicked the switch and grabbed the phone. He stared at the screen, which said 11.49pm.

Had someone died? Where the hell was the fire?

He'd forgotten to switch the phone to silent mode. Damn.

He swiped the screen and brought it to his ear.

"Hello?" he said quietly, not wanting to wake his fiancé, Gypsy, who lay unmoving in the bed beside him.

"Is this Connor? I need your help. Urgently," the woman on the other side screeched, sounding near hysteria.

Connor flinched. Great, just what he needed, a prospective client calling late on a Sunday night.

"Who is this?" He fell back into bed "Elizabeth Metcalfe. My sister's been murdered."

"Murdered? Have you called police?" said Connor.

How did this wacko find me? At that moment, he wished she'd opened the damn yellow pages and started with A for some other arse hole private investigator.

"She's disappeared," Elizabeth continued in a rush. "I'm sure she's been murdered. She left her daughter behind and she'd never do that. Never ever."

It didn't sound good. "Look, I'm sorry, Elizabeth, but it's late," he said. "Call me in the morning and we'll make an appointment."

"It's urgent. Can I come and see you in the morning first thing?"

His arms prickled up. A murder.

He let out a breath and flung back the covers. "I'm not sure. Can you call me tomorrow?"

"I wouldn't ask if I didn't really need your help. Please."

"Hang on." He padded from the bedroom to his home office and flicked on the desk light. He flicked open the pages of his paper diary and noticed he had a 2pm, but no appointments in the morning. "How about 9.45 am?"

The woman's breath blew into the handset, a sound like the fierce wind of a storm. "Thank you. I'll come then. I know your address." She paused. "I'm sorry I called so late. You probably think I'm a nut, but I'm desperate. Someone needs to do something, and the someone is you. I can't rely on police, they're overloaded."

He heard a beep as she ended the call and hung up. Making his way back to the bedroom, he dropped the mobile phone on the small table bedside table and plugged it back into the charger. Gypsy groaned quietly, shifting her feet beneath the covers, and then became still again.

She was out like a light, oblivious to the weird phone call he'd just received.

He'd assess the woman in person. The last thing he needed was another nut desperate for his help, he'd had his fair share of those in the past. He knew how to pick and choose his clients, even if his mortgage payment loomed. He had some niggling doubts about Elizabeth Metcalfe, particularly as she hadn't called police to report her sister missing yet. Most families contacted police sooner rather than later, regardless of whether their unlikable in laws worked in law enforcement. If only he hadn't lost the damn insurance contract, he could pick and choose his clients more easily.

After a trip to the bathroom, he got back into bed and turned off the light.

He gazed at the ceiling. Sleep evaded him as he tossed and turned, questions running through his mind.

If the woman's sister had been murdered, why hadn't she called the cops? She'd evaded the question, which meant either she had something to hide, or the grip of near hysteria had taken hold.

Or, her sister really had been murdered and she wouldn't tell the cops for some reason he couldn't yet figure out.

He knew he'd find out in the morning.

##

Monday Morning

Connor had fallen into the amnesia of sleep minutes after receiving the phone call, which almost removed all traces of the memory of the strange conversation the night before. Almost, but not quite.

By 9.30 a.m. he'd showered, dressed, had breakfast and helped Gypsy get their son, Mark, ready for day care. Mark wailed, annoyed, probably tired; it wasn't easy being a kid and being hauled around. Gypsy did her best, but they'd both underestimated the time and energy expended caring for an eleven-month-old. It was exhausting. He still remembered the day of Mark's birth, months after Gypsy's shooting. The joy, the relief, he'd known the day of Mark's birth that he and Gypsy would be linked forever by their son.

After a quick goodbye kiss, and a meaningful look exchanged with Gypsy he watched, as with a sigh she hoisted the scruffy blue bag with its green appliqued giraffe, up from the couch onto her shoulder and shuffled towards the back door.

The commute from living room to office took less than a minute, which meant he could set his own timetable, on his terms. Even if he was going broke on a slippery slope, the slippery slope was his. He'd rather be broke than a yes man confined by the petty bureaucracy of Victoria Police.

He waited for Elizabeth Metcalfe at his desk, tapping his pen on the dark wood. He attempted to scrutinise his home office with an objective eye. Despite the daylight, he flicked on the gun metal grey adjustable desk light. He walked around the desk, peering through the net curtains to the garden beyond. Gypsy had helped establish the informal office with a mixture of relief and trepidation after his announcement that his days in blue were over. No more political bullshit.

Something about the way Elizabeth spoke last night, her strident tone, her insistence that he intervene in the disappearance of her sister, bugged him. She seemed sure of herself for someone that had lost their marbles.

He also had the evidence back for a previous case, Mrs. Reeves, who'd engaged him to find proof of her husband's adultery. That conversation would be fun.

As he sank into the heavily cushioned brown office chair, a tapping sound, quiet and tentative, knocked on his door.

He frowned as he walked back up the three narrow steps to the hallway, walked two steps and paused before opening the main door, allowing entry to his office. A heavy-set woman stood on the second step, wearing a light grey skirt and a blue and white striped blouse with the top two buttons undone. She peered up at him, eyes squinting in the sun, a wisp of hair having emerged from her heavily lacquered do.

"Come in." Connor took a step back to allow the woman entry.

Elizabeth Metcalfe looked nothing like he imagined her. She adjusted the strap on her bag as she climbed the steep steps to the place where he stood. She was at least a foot shorter than him, about five foot five.

She didn't look like a desperate woman, but rather seemed certain of the injustice of the situation judging by the way she squared her shoulders and the grim set of her mouth. She stepped down into the office and stood next to the visitor's chair, shifting her weight from one foot to the other.

"Take a seat," he said as he settled into his chair, and then leaned back to wait.

He scrutinised her. She glanced around, folding her hands across her handbag as if forming a barrier.

She had sounded hysterical on the telephone, sure of the person responsible for her sister's disappearance, having added two and two together to make five. She'd insisted on an appointment the next morning, yet in person she rocketed between various emotions, one moment supremely confident, now unsure, rattled and out of breath.

"How can I help?" Connor said, conscious of establishing a formal tone, a professional relationship, especially with a potentially unstable client.

He didn't need a repeat of last month's performance when he'd fended off the advances of a rather busty red head, who'd used the appointment to indulge her fantasies of an affair with a private investigator, more specifically on the desk of his office with the lights dimmed. Although flattering, he wasn't interested in an easy date; he was taken. Cheap, maybe, but not easy. The woman had watched too many private eye serials and he'd told her to take her late-night fantasies elsewhere, which hadn't been received too well.

The last thing he needed was trouble, the revocation of his license. His time in law enforcement had included stints of several years on patrol, followed by a move to the drug squad, and then the criminal investigation bureau for the remainder of his career before he'd lost the hunger for police work. He figured when a detective ends up bitter and disillusioned, better to quit than start whining about it.

"I thought we covered that. I assume you assess your inquiries for interest and relevance?" The skin around her lips puckered as she spoke.

Connors skin tingled and a heaviness hit his gut. He wouldn't bite. "I do, but I wouldn't have agreed to see you if I didn't think the situation warranted it"

"I heard," Elizabeth said, the fingers on her right hand grasping at the fabric of her blouse. "I asked around. Apparently, you're one of the best, after more than a decade of loyal service. Plus, you have abilities which are, shall we say, unusual."

Shit.

How the hell did this lunatic find out he was a Sentinel? He'd been careful, and the information had been released on a need-to-know basis. He could count on one hand the people that knew, namely Gypsy, his previous illegitimate daughter Christie, and cop son-in-law, Ryan. All of them were sworn to secrecy and as far as he knew, they hadn't blabbed.

"That information is confidential. I get the job done," Connor said, raising his eyebrow and looking outside through the window next to his desk.

"I know, but this job's a bit different, and I need to know," she said.

Why did she need to know he was a Sentinel? His abilities meant he could sever a psychic connection between spirits, to guard or protect the psychic medium, especially where this became a problem, although in recent years, he'd received visions, the last one from a living person. He was conflicted enough about what he could do, without this random stranger bringing it up as a hidden benefit. If the woman's sister was alive, she'd need to work damn hard to get a message through to him. He'd only been able to receive messages from the living over recent times. Or maybe she was desperate enough, which was a distinct possibility.

All clients believed they were different, confident their case was a unique and special one, without the faintest idea of how similar their problems were.

Unfaithful spouses, business associates hell bent on betrayal, reference checks on potential employees—most clients begged for his help, confident that once provided with proof, they'd have closure to a problem niggling at their frayed lives.

The reality turned out to be the complete opposite, one for one. They resented him, as he observed from the repeated rising voices and reddened faces which occurred with almost unfailing accuracy. Most people couldn't deal with reality and refused to believe the truth, even once he showed it in black and white. At least they were consistent. They attempted to shoot the messenger, sometimes literally.

It was time to get down to business, and get this interview with Elizabeth over quickly. Connor Reardon expected a rundown on the problem at hand. She was lucky to have an urgent appointment. He wondered how many investigators would not only accept a phone call at ten to midnight, but book in an appointment less than twelve hours later.

Elizabeth's sheer persistence, reminded him of his fiancé, Gypsy Shields.

Three years earlier, he'd taken an extended leave of absence after Gypsy almost lost her life during an investigation. Strictly speaking, they didn't work together, but Gypsy had through sheer persistence, got herself involved in prior investigations. Combined with his suspension the previous year from the Victorian Police Commissioner on a trumped-up thin allegation when he'd located Joanne Seyer's, held captive at his parent's warehouse property, Connor had left in disgust. The accusation proved baseless and had eventually been thrown out but the damage was done. Combined with spending months at Gypsy's side as she recovered from a gunshot wound, he'd caved and submitted a request for a leave of absence, despite half-hearted pleadings.

The time had been right.

"I need you to do some digging" Elizabeth said.

"Go on."

"I got home Saturday, and found a message from my sister, Lauren, on my voice mail. She sounded distraught, panicky. I knew something was up straight away. She's usually so calm and organised and has the family activities planned to within an inch of their lives. She asked me if her and my niece could stay with us for a few days. But when I arrived, ready to collect them, Jarrod was home and said she'd already left, without her daughter." Elizabeth had lost most of the colour in her face, the pink tinge gone, replaced instead with an unhealthy pallor. "I asked where she'd gone and Jarrod got defensive, telling me she'd left him to take up with another man, which I don't believe for a minute. Elizabeth had never hinted at an affair, ever. She was loyal to a fault, not that he deserved it."

Maybe she had willingly disappeared. Connor waited, allowing Elizabeth to tell the rest of the tale. Getting clients to talk about private or embarrassing subjects was an art he'd unfortunately acquired with time. Although he enjoyed the perks of working for himself, occasionally the lure of a job where he didn't need to think tugged at him. A job packing boxes looked appealing about now.

He propped his right foot on his left knee, swinging his hips as he did so. "Jarrod obviously is her husband. And her daughter, you saw her?"

"Briefly. He barely opened the door. She hovered behind him looking worried and scared. My niece called out my name but by then the door was slammed shut. I'm sure the bastard is pleased about this. There never was much love lost between us."

"I see. If it's not an indelicate question, why do you need me?"

"Because he murdered her, that's why." For such a dramatic statement, Elizabeth Metcalfe seemed unperturbed, feathers barely ruffled. Her perfectly coiffed hair didn't move as she turned her head. Her handbag, reflected the sunlight streaming in through the front window.

"What makes you so sure of that? That's a fairly serious accusation."

"I'm fully aware of that fact. He claimed her things were gone and she'd left a note." She snorted. "We all know any idiot can forge a Dear John letter. If anyone was capable of something this evil, it's that worm. I never trusted him, not from the first time I met him. He isn't right in the head. He's dodgy, rotten to the core."

He stayed silent, unsure how to respond.

"Lauren would never leave her daughter, ever, I know she wouldn't."

"A lot of people say what they think they should say. Unfortunately, some parents do leave children behind if they're leaving an unbearable marriage."

Elizabeth's face went red, and she lifted her behind up from the seat temporarily before sitting back down with a thump. "Not my Lauren! Never, ever! We talked about it, after a friend of ours left her husband."

"Did Lauren speculate?"

"What do you mean, speculate?"

Connor ran his fingers through his hair. Elizabeth

just couldn't accept that her sister would up and leave without a word. Rather than engage his services to track her down, she'd be better off hiring a counsellor. The last thing he needed right now was a loose cannon.

"Guessing. Maybe she told you what she would do in a similar situation."

"Oh, I see." Elizabeth fiddled with a pendant around her neck, a silver moon. "Well, she said that she couldn't understand why anyone would leave their child behind, especially if the partner was difficult." She paused, glaring at Connor, daring him to interrupt her. "She said that husbands come and go, but children are forever."

He wanted to say, don't hold back lady, say what you think, but thought better of it. No good alienating a potentially well-paying client until she'd said her piece.

He rearranged the papers on his desk, straightening the edges of an unruly pile.

He cleared his throat. "Well, Elizabeth, my rates are here, although being a woman who obviously does her research before hiring an investigator, I'm sure you already know them."

He pushed a sheet of paper across to her. She picked it up carefully, eyebrows raised.

She glanced at it before placing it back on the desk, looking back at him. "You're right. I'm aware of your rates. If we're going to work together, though, we need to clear something up. I get the impression you think I'm nuts."

"Sorry?" Connor loosened his tie.

"You know a screw loose, a sandwich short of a picnic, the lights are on and nobody is—"

"I'm familiar with the term. Look, there's a simple explanation for what's happened. Your sister left an unhappy marriage. I understand that she left your niece behind, which is surprising, shocking even, but I'm sure if you approach family services or the courts you can begin the process to gain access to your niece."

"But that could take months! By then, it will be too late, much too late. I need answers. We all do. My parents, they're frail, and this has been very hard on them. Mum had a stroke last year and Dad has heart problems. They're talking about a pacemaker now. If Lauren isn't found soon, I hate to think what will happen..." Her gaze wandered from him, to the desk, to the piece of paper lying forlorn and unwanted on the desk.

He didn't like the way the conversation was going. "I'm sorry, but as I'm sure you are aware, this is more of a police matter, rather than something I can help with. I'm assuming you or her husband have reported her missing?"

"That's the whole problem. I plan to, but I haven't. The report would be lost for sure, ignored or filed in the circular file. A complete waste of time."

What an idiot.

Connor's chin dipped, and he turned from side to side on the office chair. Even though he'd attempted to knock her back, she wouldn't give up.

"How so? I can assure you the police are pretty thorough, considering what they have to work with."

Like lunatic dysfunctional families.

"I'm sure they are. The straight ones, that is."

"I'm not following."

"That's the whole reason I came to you. I thought you knew that. Lauren's excuse for a husband, Jarrod Whitehouse, the old bastard, is a Senior Sergeant at eastern region police headquarters."

###

CHAPTER 2

Being decidedly hungry, Connor knew he'd take on the case. Plus, the cat was out of the bag regarding his Sentinel abilities, so it made sense to use them for a client who'd deliberately searched him out. Something was off in the woman's disappearance, primarily the fact that the missing woman's husband was a senior member of police, combined with her husband's belief that she'd run off with her lover.

As a member of police, her husband had a duty to report her missing, unless of course, he didn't want colleagues to know about it. Probably an old-school cop who didn't want anyone to know he had a life. He knew the type; kids should be seen and not heard and women belonged in the kitchen. Hell, he'd run away if forced to live with someone like that. Plus, this was the first case he could remember as an investigator where it bordered on a criminal matter, a chance to use his skills as a detective.

He would hunt for evidence, especially for a client willing to foot the bill.

"If I'm going to take on the case, I'll need more information," he said.

"Such as?"

"Well, some basic info to start with." He pushed a form toward Elizabeth. "Full name, address, date of birth, employment details, and car registration."

"Okay." She pulled the form across the desk, picked up a pen, and began scratching out Lauren's basic information.

"Social media details will help, also. I'll leave you to fill that out, then I'll come back and we'll talk for a bit longer. Can I get you a cup of tea or coffee?" Feeling generous, he decided the woman had money, and was nothing if not sold on his capabilities.

Elizabeth scribbled busily, and then momentarily lifted her head managing a halfhearted smile. "That would be lovely. Tea, white and one sugar, please."

She went back to the form.

Connor got up from his desk, climbed up the three steps, and headed for the kitchen. Gypsy remained, head down over her laptop on the dining room table, and he flicked on the kettle, preparing tea in two mugs. As the water boiled, he wondered about the case. A weird one. Sure, the husband and sister's reasons sounded plausible—Jarrod because he knew she'd left him and didn't want the embarrassment of alerting others; Elizabeth because she wasn't convinced of the integrity of the missing persons department—but none of it rang true. Most family members would report a disappearance, at least twenty-four hours afterward, many of them attempting it sooner due to anxiety and worry. The only person that seemed anxious here was her sister. Where the hell was everybody else?

He wanted to run his musings past Gypsy, but remained quiet for now. His prospective client would probably overhear. Collecting the two mugs from the bench, he headed back to his desk, taking care not to slop the tea onto the floor as he went.

Back in his office, he bent at the knees and placed the mug of tea beside his soon-to-be client.

"Thank you," Elizabeth said, putting down her pen.

Connor took a seat at the other side of the desk. "I'm interested in your sister's movements. When was the last time you saw her?"

"Well, other than the phone call a few days ago, I last saw her two weeks ago, at our parents' place for a family get together."

"Did you notice any change in her behavior? Different appearance or mood?"

"Not really. She did talk about being worried about the finances after they refinanced the house. Renovations, apparently. But she'd seemed to perk up, happier than usual over the last few weeks."

"What does she do for work?"

"She's a sales administrator at Brentwood plastics. Part time, three days a week." Elizabeth took a small sip of tea.

Obviously, she'd be absent from work. Time to take up another aspect.

"Is she active on social media?" Connor said.

"Not really." Elizabeth wiped her hands on her skirt. "Maybe once a fortnight, if that. Obviously, she hasn't posted for a while, but then that bastard's done god knows what to her." She spoke through gritted teeth.

"Well, if you can report her missing today, the

police will investigate, and so will I. It really is the fastest way to track her down."

"If Laura has run away with some random guy, as Jarrod wants us to believe, why leave her car behind?'

"She didn't take it with her?"

"No. It's parked in her driveway. I drove past there today and saw it still in the driveway. If you were going to run off and have an affair, would you leave your car behind?"

"Probably not. I'll start with tracing her last movements, who saw her, finances, work, social media, that type of thing."

"Good. Here's the information you asked for." Elizabeth pushed the form back to him. "It goes without saying if you have any other questions, you should call me, day or night. My sister means the world to me, to all of us."

"I will" he said, his mind already working through various possibilities.

Elizabeth stood up from her chair, grasping her handbag with tight white fingers.

"You'll report her missing today?" he said.

She frowned. "I said I will."

"Call another station if that makes you more comfortable. Here are my bank details with an approximate bill—a deposit will get the ball rolling." He handed her an invoice.

"Thank you. I'll process a payment when I get back to the computer at home."

She took the invoice and left the office, taking with her the sad remnants of a broken family.

After bidding her goodbye and closing the door, Connor headed through the doorway to enter the living area. Perhaps, if the wind blew the right way, he could run recent events by Gypsy, get her take on things, as they had in days gone by. Her ability to communicate with the dead made her useful, because if Lauren had been murdered, Gypsy would be the conduit through which he could talk to the victim.

He stepped through the L-shaped lounge room, dominated by the large painting on the wall, a feature they'd purchased just prior to the birth of their first child together Mark, a gift to themselves. At the time, it had signified a new chapter for them, a turning point, featuring buds amongst the bush, a beautiful cottage with a background of green and blue hills.

Gypsy was hunched over the laptop, her dark silky brown hair a veil. She bit at her lip as she pecked at the keys.

He stood with feet apart, directly in her line of sight, waiting for her to look up.

She didn't, or wouldn't.

He shoved his hands in his pockets, shifting his weight to his right hip. "Gypsy?"

She raised her head, hooking a section of dark brown hair over her right ear. "What?"

Like rose petals hanging on past their bloom, a gust of wind would send her flying off in any direction.

"That client knew I was a Sentinel."

She lifted her head. "Well, don't stare at me. I didn't blab. I'm practically climbing the walls, we rarely socialise these days, and I don't think Ryan or Christie are exactly gossips."

"Yeah," he said, hands on hips. "How did she find out then?"

"I don't know. Maybe you could add on a Sentinel surcharge?"

"Hilarious."

"I'm serious. You think it's a dirty secret, something to fade into the background, but most people, like me, know it's a valuable skill."

The last thing he wanted to do was open that can of worms, having asked his fiancé to keep a lid on her own abilities after she'd been shot. She shifted her focus back to the laptop.

He pulled back the dark brown chair back and slid onto it. He rested his forearms on the table and focused to give her his full attention.

"I need your help." He kept his tone quiet and, he hoped, neutral.

"What's new?" She had gone back to not looking at him.

"What's going on?"

"Nothing."

The silence stretched between them, until it became a thing, a buzzing mass of energy.

"Mrs. Reeves will be here in an hour. Helen Reeves. I thought we could have lunch, then you'd sit in the office with me while she's here."

Gypsy looked at him, and her chair scraped back a few inches across the tiled floor. She spread fingers of both hands across the table.

"I'll go make lunch." He mumbled.

They'd been together for more than four years now and in that time, he'd learned when to pick his battles.

He headed back to the kitchen and opened the fridge door without really seeing what was in there.

Shaking his head, he grabbed some ham, cheese, onions, and pasta. If he focused on the here and now, he'd get to the bottom of whatever was bugging her.   He'd known of her tendency to fly off the handle when they met, but since Mark had come along, the same tendency had grown from an occasional quirk to a full-blown annoyance.

Finding a saucepan, he boiled some water on a slow heat as he chopped the ham and onion. He did his best to push away speculation and stay in the present.

"I'm sorry." She said. "It's just...life."

She covered her face with her hands.

He wondered if she'd had enough sleep but now was not the time to ask.

"I know you feel guilty and you didn't want to do it, but it's for the best, I promise."

"It's not about putting Mark in child care." Her eyes filled.

"What is it then?" he said.

"You shouldn't have asked me to do it. It's too much," she said, pulling her hands away from her face, which looked pale and empty.

"Do what?"

"Suppress my abilities, push them down. I get it. I was reckless, selfish, and put myself in harm's way, but that was the past. You can't keep punishing me forever. We have a son now, a beautiful boy. No way do I want to leave you or him."

"Watching you in intensive care after the shooting, the rehab, was...rough."

"I've said sorry so many times, and spent the last eighteen months trying to make it up to you. But like I said to you the night we met, it's not like a tap, I can't just turn it on and off at will."

"I need you with me. I can't lose you again." His fingers clenched into a fist so he moved them under the table.

"You won't, I promise. Either you lose me suddenly, which won't happen again, or we keep going like this, a slow and painful erosion, constant unexpressed resentment. What I can do is part of me, and you're asking me to withhold all of that. I can't do it anymore. It's coming between us."

"I need time," he said. "Let me digest it, think about it some more."

"Okay."

"We'll work it out. I promise, in the end, everything will be all right."

"It doesn't feel like it." She turned her face to look at him, her eyes pleading.

"It probably doesn't. But it doesn't change the fact that I love you."

He walked over and stood behind her and put both hands on her shoulders. Reaching around, he kissed her gently on the cheek. She wiped underneath her eyes, elbows on the table, running her fingers down her face.

Connor moved back to the kitchen to focus on lunch prep. He figured if she ate, she'd be more rational. He could only hope.

He turned off the pasta, put down the knife, washed his hands, and sat back down again at the table.

"I like having you in the office with me," he said.

"I know. It's just...I don't know."

"Mrs. Reeves might scream, fall off her chair, bawl, throw herself on the ground who knows. The news isn't good. You know the drill," Connor said.

"I wish I didn't. I'm not in the mood to babysit your clients today."

"Okay."

"I feel terrible. Mark shouldn't be in child care. But it's not just that. I can't keep going on like this. Just because I can't do anything about it, doesn't mean the visions have stopped. "

Connor got up from the chair and stood beside her, but she barely moved.

"Come here," he said.

She seemed to contemplate whether she would get up. She raised her head, eyes wide, and after a few seconds something in his expression must have convinced her. She scraped the chair back, and stood up. Connor stepped forward and took her in his arms, holding her. She allowed him to hug her for a few seconds, no more, and then pushed him away.

Her eyes had filled.

"I know it doesn't seem like it right now, but we'll get through this," he said quietly.

"Will we? That was never what I imagined when I dreamed of us getting married and having kids."

"Me either, but things will get better."

Gypsy didn't answer, and Connor figured he'd helped her for now. If not, she'd have to sulk until Helen Reeves left.

He moved back from the dining room into the kitchen. "I do need your help."

Gypsy sighed.

He drained the pasta. "My client might freak out. You know how they get when I have evidence. She'll react, I just don't know how."

"You can handle it."

"Like I handled that red head, what was her name, Sybil?"

He turned his head in Gypsy's direction and was

rewarded with a smirk.

"Oh, you remembered her name huh? So, who's the client this arvo, did you say Helen?"

"That's her, Helen Reeves."

"Middle aged?"

"Yeah."

She laughed out loud. "Well, I hardly think a middle-aged woman will throw herself at you."

"You'd be surprised."

"I know I think you're gorgeous but not every single woman that meets you feels the same." She sat up straighter. "Only ninety-nine percent of them."

"I'm not good with weeping, screaming women."

"You think I am?"

"All I'm asking is that you sit with me in the office. A few feet away as backup will do. I don't need a complaint, neither of us do. If I lose my license, we're screwed."

Gypsy got up from the table and walked over to stand next to him on his left. She rubbed his back from the curve of his spine to the top a couple of times.

"These conversations still worry me," he said.

"Even after three years, or whatever it is?"

"Yep."

"How long do you think it'll take?"

"I don't know, maybe half an hour? I'll get straight to the point."

"You usually do. Remember, I've got my own work to get through. I'll bill you for my time."

Connor paused with a block of cheese in his right hand to look at her. "Hang on a—"

"Gotcha." She pushed herself up on her toes and kissed him on the cheek, and then walked back to the dining table. She sat back on the chair, looking at her laptop. She wiggled on the seat.

He pressed his lips together. Cheeky woman. Lucky, he liked her a bit. Or maybe more than a bit.

Leaning down, he took two bowls from the cupboard, emptied the pasta into them, followed by ham and cheese. Plain and basic, just the way he liked it. He gave it a quick stir and headed for the dining table where Gypsy sat, laptop ignored.

"Thanks for making lunch." She took her bowl.

"No problem."

Unspoken words hung in the air, a cloud of buzzing vapour.

They ate in silence for a few moments.

"What time's this Helen arriving?" Gypsy asked.

Connor dropped the fork and checked the silver watch on his wrist. "Two o'clock. Twenty minutes."

"Okay." She finished chewing and then said, "So, what evidence you got?"

"Photos."

"Of what? Him caught in the act with some other chick? Busty red head by any chance?" She smirked.

"My sides are splitting."

Rather than expressing shock or upset when he'd told her about the prospective client coming on to him six months ago, Gypsy had laughed and hugged him, while he remained rigid. He counted himself lucky the stupid bird hadn't taken it further, due to lack of witnesses. If a client reported him, sued, or sought to get his license revoked, they'd be in the financial mud. Gypsy told him not to stress, which didn't help. Apparently, her theory was that by worrying about it, he'd make it happen which struck him as complete bullshit. She didn't seem to grasp that a disaster like that would ruin them, but then the financial pressure lay primarily on him.

He gazed at her as she finished the last of her lunch, and realised how far they'd come in nearly four years together, but also how much they hadn't known when they'd moved in together. They should have talked about the important issues like money, children, child care, the practical matters. In the early days, they'd gone with the flow, pushed along on the sea of hope and happiness, confident it would all work out, love would conquer all, which turned out to be a crock. Yeah, love was important, but it took more than love to sort issues out. It took patience and persistence, traits that weren't exactly at the top of his list.

"So, are you going to tell me, or enjoy while I suffer the pain of anticipation?" Gypsy said, fork poised in front of her face.

"I did catch Mr. Reeves in the act, but not with a busty brunette."

"Oh yeah?" Gypsy dropped her fork into her bowl and sat up straighter, lunch finished.

"I followed him to Chapel Street. I took photos from the car of him kissing and groping another man."

Gypsy gasped. "Another man?"

"It happens."

She rubbed at her chin. "Well, yeah, I guess it does, but it's the first time you've found a bloke with another bloke, isn't it?"

"Yeah, especially a usually conservative type. Joe Reeves is a Project Manager by day and closet bisexual after hours."

"Sheesh. You would've thought he'd be more

careful if he didn't want his wife to know. Or maybe this is his way of telling her. Not exactly tactful."

Connor checked his watch. "We'll find out soon."

Gypsy slid the bowls across the table. He stood, heading toward his office. As he reached the hallway, the front door bell rang. He opened the front door and she stood on the top step, a well-groomed, slim, middle aged blonde.

"Mrs. Reeves." He smiled. "Come in, please."

"Thank you." She smiled back and headed through to his office.

"Take a seat, I'll be with you in a moment." Connor turned and made for the kitchen, where Gypsy had resumed her post at the table, eyes riveted to the laptop screen.

He leaned over and whispered inches from her ear, "She's here, in the office. You ready?"

Gypsy brushed the front of her top and sighed. "She's early."

"You look fine," he whispered, taking her hand to guide her toward the office. "Let's go."

Gypsy stood, blowing out a breath, and he let go of her hand. She followed him to his office.

Mrs. Reeves sat tightly on the chair, clenching her hands together tightly.

Gypsy moved to sit to the right of Mrs. Reeves, about two feet away.

"I hope you don't mind, but I asked my fiancé, Gypsy, to sit in with us. I find sometimes a woman's touch can help with news of this type," he said.

"So, it's bad then." Helen's voice sounded huskier than he remembered it. She cleared her throat.

"Well, I do have evidence. I followed Joe for some time, I have a series of photos. There's no easy way to prepare you for this. He may be having an affair."

Gypsy flicked a look at Connor and Helen swallowed hard, a visible lump in her throat shifting downward like a tough piece of beef.

"I'd like to see them."

"Before you see them, you should know, your husband is having an affair possibly with another man."

"What?" Mrs. Reeves' voice cracked.

Connor opened the top drawer of a cabinet to the right of the desk, removed a file and placed it on the desk. Helen Reeves' gaze followed his hands as he opened the file to reveal several enlarged photographs. He picked up the first two and looked at them. He'd taken them from his phone when parked a way down from the club, and had managed a series of roughly twenty shots. Only four of them were clear enough to see faces but there was no mistaking Mr. Joseph Reeves, engaged in a passionate kiss with another man, who looked a fair bit younger.

Gypsy turned her legs around so she faced the side of the client's chair. Mrs. Reeves' attention remained riveted on the photos in Connor's hand. He reached forward and left them on the outer edge of the desk, inches away from her.

Mrs. Reeves picked up the photos and stared at them without blinking for what seemed like an eternity but was probably only ten seconds. She closed her eyes and let out a deep breath. Once her eyes opened, she giggled.

Connor met Gypsy's gaze. Most clients after receiving bad news, either ran like terrified animals from his office, often before he'd finished giving them the information in full. Others became silent, their reddened faces and tense muscles a ticking time bomb. Some exploded, and others went into hysterics in his office.

But it looked like in Mrs. Reeves case this was a non-event. Thank God.

"Is this all? A kiss with another man?" She laughed, a breathy gush of relief. "I imagined the worst, a young blonde or maybe he'd got someone pregnant. But this? This is not as bad as I thought, experimentation, nothing more."

Connor flicked a glance at Gypsy. She looked as dazed and incredulous as him. In nearly three years, he hadn't encountered this. Did Mrs. Reeves worry about status and what others thought? Just when he thought he had people figured out, something like this happened.

Human nature. After more than a decade in the police force and now more than two years as a private detective, he thought he'd seen and heard it all. The darkest of violence, gruesome murders, and savagery. But this insistence on remaining a married woman, the idea that somehow her husband having it off with a bloke didn't count, shocked him. The desperate necessity of maintaining the status quo rankled.

"So, you're not bothered by this?" Gypsy said.

Connor glared at her, sending her what he hoped was the shut-up signal, to stay out of it. She didn't look back at him, so she hadn't got the message. She'd been a psychic there for a while, jumping in during investigations and although her heart was in the right place, she'd been almost killed. His own Sentinel abilities had resurfaced for a while, but they'd both turned the switch off so hard there it had been more than two years since either one of them relied on mental communication. Besides, all he did as a Sentinel was intercept spirit communication, usually from psychic to spirit, and in at least one case it had been for the better. The whole thing however remained little consolation compared to the risk of other cops finding out about him. Possible fall out from a damaged reputation if word got out meant he'd put a dampener on his abilities as a way to get through each day.

Mrs. Reeves' nervous laugh had subsided, and she'd put the photographs back on the desk. Colour rose in her face. "No, I'm not. It's just a kiss, probably a one off with a man. Experimentation and curiosity. Nothing more."

Connor knew it was more than a kiss. He'd seen them grope each other and disappear hand in hand. He had photos for that too, but left them in the file until he could get a better idea of response. He wouldn't shatter the woman's illusions further. It would possibly piss her off, not to mention her husband and he didn't want the problem of an unpaid bill, either. So, he left it undisclosed.

"You might be right," he said. He shifted in his chair. "Here's the bill. Can you make payment by bank deposit?"

Mrs. Reeves smiled and reached for her phone. "Yes, I'll do a bank transfer now. I have your bank details."

"Sorry, but you're going to stay married—" Gypsy began.

Connor put a hand up to quiet her. "Anyway, I'm sure you're busy, Mrs. Reeves. Once you've processed payment, I'll issue a receipt. I hope I was of some service to you."

Her smile widened.

"Yes, thank you." She finished tapping on her phone and held up the screen to show Connor. "I've just put through an online banking payment. Thank you again for all your hard work, Mr. Reardon. I can move on now."

Mrs. Reeves stood up and turned. Gypsy tried the look of death but it wouldn't work on him. She would be the first to complain if they couldn't pay the bills. She'd have to suck it up.

He followed Mrs. Reeves to the front door and closed it behind her. He stepped down into the office to peer through the window, checking she was back in the car before turning to Gypsy. As usual, her hair crackled with nuclear fission, and her hand was out, ready to begin with her ridiculous hand gestures and pointing that came with every argument.

Here we go.

"You liar, dirty rotten liar."

Connor sighed and headed for the kitchen to make coffee.

"What did you want me to do?" He said without looking back at her. "Show her the picture of her husband groping another guy? Of them heading off hand in hand to a hotel room? Would that have made you happy?"

"Don't start. You know exactly what I'm talking about. You lied to her to keep the peace. Her husband is screwing someone else, and you didn't tell her because you're worried about her paying the precious bill!" The muscles in her cheek tightened and her teeth were clenched. She had almost hit full flight, anger peaking.

"So, what? I can't win with you. If I'd told her the truth, you would've been pissed off I upset her and I'd talked you into helping me pick up the pieces. She paid a deposit but wouldn't have paid the final bill and then you'd crack the shits. Seriously, what do I have to do to win with you?"

"You make me sound like the worst woman in the world." The pitch of her voice had lowered from hysterical anger to loud antagonism, and her hands had dropped to her side.

Connor knew better than to bite. He turned to her and looked her in the eye. "I'm damned if I do and damned if I don't."

He wondered what had happened to them. They'd been together five years, living together for nearly three, and since they'd started a family it had all changed. The pressure, the annoying habits, it wasn't fun anymore. They didn't talk the way they used to, didn't laugh or spend much quality time together.

Gypsy sat down heavily on the couch, her hands over her face for a second. She pulled them away. "But you're the one always going on about liability, legal cases waiting to happen, and you're terrified you'll lose your license. If you keep on banging on about it, it'll happen, a self-fulfilling prophecy."

Connor sat down beside her. The silence stretched between them.

"I'm tired, exhausted and it's only two thirty." Said Gypsy

"Me, too."

Another longish silence.

"So, what are you going to do about Mrs. Reeves?" Gypsy had rocketed from fury to antagonism and now to calming down in a matter of seconds.

"Leave it. She doesn't want change, happy with the status quo. Helen Reeves has paid the bill and moved on."

Gypsy rested her hand on the couch seat beside her. "Aren't you shocked by what just happened?"

Connor paused. "A bit."

She shook her head. He knew she didn't understand. He was stunned too, but he was aware that seemingly respectable citizens hid all sorts of secrets. He had been surprised by the client's reaction, but he despaired more about his own marriage. However, he couldn't or wouldn't show that to Gypsy. It would mean weakness. Surely, she knew that?

How would he tell her of his terror at not providing for her? That he somehow sensed the gap between them growing by tiny increments day by day, a chasm of inky darkness.

"But how can she live like that?" Gypsy continued. "Do you think she knows he's sleeping with a man? Even if it's kissing, that's bad enough. How does something like that not devastate her?"

"It probably does, but she can't show it or risk public humiliation. She doesn't want her settled life to change."

A long silence again. It rolled around like a mass of swirling dust mites.

Gypsy stood up and moved closer to him, less than a foot away. Her face was beautiful, even during an argument. Those eyes held him every time, mesmerising.

"I guess our life could be worse." She grabbed him gently by his shirt front, pulling him forward just enough for her to kiss him. The sweet scent of her breath wafted over.

"It could. One of us could be sleeping with another man." His mouth twisted. "And I know it's not me."

She smiled. "I don't doubt it. One is more than enough for me."

She got up and walked away. She had never been great at affection at the best of times, and even more so after a fight. He should have kissed her but the hard-sharp communication almost knocked him over. The pot of anger had simmered down to a low bubble rather than a furious boil.

Why couldn't he break out of his mould, the god forsaken cage of being a man? A lifetime of training, that's why. His mother had brought him up tough. Left by her husband when Connor was nine years old, Casey Reardon had done her best under the circumstances. That included no money, and a case of overwhelming anger that hardened her shell.

Casey Reardon, despite keeping her married name, loathed her ex-husband with vicious intensity, nattering about him to burst the boil of caustic poison Connor somehow knew as a child had invaded her entire body.

Couldn't Gypsy see that? Why didn't she understand? She'd been a psychic years ago, but had stopped at his insistence during their final venomous battle. Interfering in his police investigations to find criminals had helped at times, but once it got her shot and lingering at death's door, there was no going back to her old ways.

He'd delivered an ultimatum.

Turn off the psychic lever, hard, or lose him forever. Thankfully, she'd chosen him.

So how could he now tell her that he wanted her to backpedal, to reverse the switch, so she could see his innermost pictures nestled within his mental filing cabinets, lurking at the back covered in dust?

He couldn't. Plus, there was the other factor which swirled around inside his skull, and he didn't dare pin it down in case he'd have to look at it too hard. As a Sentinel, a guard, he could and had in the past, blocked psychic signals including hers.

She could read minds and talk to the dead but couldn't read his, so he let her walk away. One day, just maybe, there'd be a meeting of minds again, but until then, he'd be content with what he had. A son, the son he'd dreamed of, a gorgeous fiancé who still loved him, and a job that he didn't mind, even if now second best to his former years in the force.

Ryan, his son in law and only contact in the police force would understand the pressure and possibly have information on the Lauren Whitehouse case. He'd call him. Soon.

###

CHAPTER 3

Doing his best to erase his last appointment with Helen Reeves from his mind, Connor reset himself mentally, set his shoulders back, and looked at the clean slate of the Lauren Whitehouse investigation. He'd begun a case folder, and although most investigators conducted most of the work via computer, there was something to be said for notebook and pen to get the investigatory juices flowing. As he began to write, his phone pinged with a quiet ring to alert him to a voice mail message.

When he'd called earlier, Connor got the voicemail greeting for Ryan Sheehan, his brother in law, Senior Constable in the Criminal Investigation Division at Carlton police station. The vapour of nostalgia for his days in the force had largely vanished although not completely, replaced by a grim acceptance, a determination to go it alone. He grimaced.

The message on his phone was probably Ryan returning his call.

Connor bit down on the end of a pen. Calling his

brother in law Ryan had been the easy option, a Sergeant in his old station, Carlton, but Ryan didn't know Jarrod Whitehouse personally.

The answer just might be Cliff Jenson. Cliff had retired four years earlier and Connor hadn't stayed in touch, but that was how life rolled. He and Cliff had always got along. Big Cliff, as he was known, had gone through more scrapes than he could count, but somehow emerged unscathed. Cliff was one of the good ones, a genuine nice guy, and the bureaucracy of the force irritated him even more than it did Connor.

Cliff had cut corners, roughed up suspects who'd later complained, and pissed off the wrong people. Somehow, despite the enquiries, and internal affairs investigations he'd managed to stay in the force. Connor didn't mind; Cliff was a genuinely nice guy and if his actions were viewed by some as questionable, particularly the weasels in internal affairs, Cliff's motives were always the right ones, the supreme test as far as he was concerned. Too many cops had forgotten that part of their job involved getting off their arses and knocking on doors, to put the bad guys where they belonged.

Cliff had divorced over a decade ago and over drinks one night had talked about it, unheard of for most cops who were renowned for internalising job stress. He'd been drunk enough to tell his story, the despair, his anger, hopelessness, and grief that he'd probably never see his son again, who at that stage was only twelve. The marriage was Cliff's second, and this time he'd married a much younger woman, obviously, a gold digger, not that anyone dared mention it to him.

Connor remembered their last meeting. They'd

arranged to catch up at the Sportsman's Arms Hotel in Richmond, a dingy old pub with sticky bottle green carpets and no trace of trendiness. He suspected the venue had been chosen due to its lack of popularity with cops. Jenson wasn't exactly known for his tendency as a social butterfly.

Connor's eyes had adjusted from the searing sunlight to the dark bar. He'd scanned the room and spotted Jenson in a booth in the far corner.

Connor stood beside the booth where Jensen was bent over his beer.

Jenson turned to him, eyes rounded. He managed a faint smile. Although the pub stunk of hops and stale cigarette smoke, Jenson attempted to shuffle out of the booth to greet him. Connor knew from his breath that he'd been drinking for quite a while, possibly most of the day and it was early on a Sunday afternoon.

"Don't get up, mate." Connor gestured with his left hand and sat down on the cracked red vinyl bench seat opposite him.

Jenson looked back down at his half empty beer glass, and then cupped it with both hands.

"What's happening?" Connor said.

Although Jenson had met with him after hours in the past, to exchange information about a case, that had been a long time ago. He wasn't sure if this was a personal call rather than one to exchange work information.

"Turned to shit," Jenson mumbled, so much so that Connor wondered if he'd heard him correctly.

"What's turned to shit?"

"My life, that's what." Connor thought Jensen's face might fall into the glass, or slam dangerously onto the grey and red flecked Formica table top.

Connor paused, sensing a response wasn't required. The last thing he wanted to do was stop him mid flow. Apparently, he needed to talk.

"The bitch left me." Jenson brought his head up, and only now did Connor see the bloodshot watery eyes, the grey stubble, and the haunted look on Jenson's cavernous face. "Took Noah with her. Left me a note."

"I'm sorry." The hoarseness in his voice struck him as appropriate to the situation somehow.

Maybe his colleague would sense his solidarity. He'd certainly proved himself in days gone by, which was obviously why he'd chosen Connor to offload to.

"Yeah, me too. Says she doesn't love me anymore." He brought his hands up and ran his fingers through tousled hair. "We've been together fifteen years. Who wakes up one day and decides they don't love their other half anymore?"

Connor's stomach tightened, a hardened ball of sharp glass. He had no idea what to say. He was no expert on women, far from it.

"Have you contacted your ex?"

"Tried her mobile and her parent's places. Mobile's switched off and her parents reckon they don't know where Vicky or Noah is, which is bullshit." Jensen's words were now noticeably slurred.

Connor paused again, out of his depth.

"They could be dead for all I know," Jensen continued. "Her parents are lying through their arses, but then they never liked me. My life is down the toilet."

Connor wanted to tell Jensen he still had something to live for, that he could try and get custody, that maybe Vicky would come back, but the words seemed hollow in his mind, not worth saying.

"You wouldn't...do anything stupid?" Connor, without realising it, had mirrored Jensen's body language, hands face down on the table.

"You mean top myself? Well, I'm drunk enough to tell you I thought about it. Any cop that says he hasn't is lying"

"Come stay with us, Cliff."

Jensen met his gaze. They didn't speak, and the silence highlighted the loud conversations of fellow patrons which echoed through the bar.

"I don't need your help, mate, but I appreciate it. I need someone to listen, and you were always good at that."

And so, Connor listened to Jenson tell him that his life was over and that if he couldn't ever see his son again, he didn't want to live anymore. His friend spilled his guts, until an hour and six drinks later Connor made sure his old friend got in a taxi in the hope of getting him home in one piece.

Jensen had called him months later, telling him he'd been recommended for counselling, with the department issuing a slap on the wrist for drinking on the job. Vicky the ex had divorced him, and Jensen had eventually got custody once every second weekend, although it had taken a year and a half. They'd kept in touch even if only for Jenson to tell him about the jarring reality of child custody logistics.

When he'd had been called in to give a character reference as part of his later internal enquiry, Connor had gone in to bat for Jensen. He heard later via the grapevine that after retirement, Cliff had moved out to Phillip Island, a seaside suburb nearly a two hours' drive from Brunswick where Connor lived. The Jenson family home had been sold off as part of the divorce. Connor hoped Cliff had spent his days fishing off a pier somewhere. He'd been to the retirement party years earlier but hadn't been in touch as much since then. He figured Cliff would understand part of life meant that he didn't stay in touch with a lot of the gang from the old days in CID.

After more than forty years' service in the force, Jensen knew most of the cops and had watched them come and go. Connor wanted to call Cliff and find out what he knew about Jarrod Whitehouse.

If Jarrod had a reputation as a bent or even slightly bent cop, Cliff would know.

Connor did a search on his mobile for Cliff's number. He was sure he had saved it there. Yep, there it was, a land line number.

Rather than pick up the clunky beige handset, he pressed the screen of his mobile and dialled.

It rang and rang. Cliff clung to old habits, resenting technology, and didn't agree with things like mobile telephones or having a voice mail greeting which he told Connor were sign of society's decay.

On the tenth ring, a gravelly voice said, "Hello?"

"Cliff? Cliff Jenson?"

"Who's this?"

"Connor Reardon. We used to—"

"Reardon! I remember you, old bastard. How the hell are ya?"

Connor smirked at the rough warmth in Jenson's voice.

"Not bad. How about you?" Connor smiled. He stood from his desk chair and began walking toward the front porch so he could look through the blinds and get a sense of space, as the room had closed in on him. "I'm a PI now, and I'm married. We had a boy, Mark, he's almost one."

Jensen coughed. "Gone for the big money, eh? Good on ya, mate, things worked out for you, hey? You officially resigned?"

"Well...kind of a leave of absence which became a resignation, yeah."

"Hmm. Doesn't surprise me. The brass doesn't give a damn about cops on the ground, too far up their own arses. It's been a while since we talked, let me guess...you rang me for old times' sake?"

Jensen wasn't stupid. He probably figured that if Connor had called him out of the blue, he wanted help, more than likely something out of the ordinary.

He wasn't wrong.

"I need a favour. Do you remember Jarrod Whitehouse?"

"That snake, yeah, I remember him. I hope he's deeper in dog shit than an old bloody boot" Jensen coughed again.

Connor needed to get inside Jarrod's head, to know what made him tick. It would make a difference in understanding the state of their marriage, and why Lauren might have left.

"Oh, yeah, why do you say that?" Connor shifted as he peeked out of the blinds.

"Just rumours, mate. You know how it is. He was always a rude prick back in the CID days, knew better than everyone else, not big on cooperation."

"And the rumours?"

"That he smacked his wife around, never proved. At some of the social dos, his wife seemed nervous and withdrawn, and when she spoke, he gave her the look of death. Vicky and I wondered if he smacked her around, or controlled her every word."

"But no proof, huh?"

"Nah. Couldn't stand him on sight, arrogant prick. Didn't go out of my way to talk to him, and avoided him like the plague. But a couple of times we needed to work together, share info, and the arrogant bastard treated me like a brainless junior constable. Over the years, he'd pissed more people off than you could poke a stick at. So, is he in the shit then? I hope so."

Connor's slow smile had built from budding to fully fledged. "Maybe, maybe not. His wife went missing a week ago, and her sister thinks he killed her. She asked me to investigate."

Cliffs voice dropped. "Murdered? Lauren was a good one, hard to believe. Be good to see him behind bars, but wife killer...Not so sure."

"That's why I called. I figured if anyone knew the guy, you would."

"Follow up the wife beating path, mate. He's a dodgy prick no doubt."

"Thanks. I'll visit him soon, and I'll expect a hostile response."

The cough, which at first sounded like a tickle, was now fully-fledged. Connor wondered if Jenson had given up smoking.

"Connor, it goes without saying but if I can help you, mate, I will. I'll ask around and let you know if I hear anything. Maybe I'll drive over there and catch up."

"Be good to see you. Thanks for the info, mate. Talk soon." Connor tapped the screen and hung up.

He sat back on the office chair. Time to power up

the software. He moved the mouse and the screen sprang to life. He shifted on the chair, anticipation building, and clicked on the Icon for the IntQuery software.

Okay, Jarrod, if you're up to something, I'll find out about it.

Although Elizabeth had given him the address for the Whitehouse family, he wanted to confirm it. He typed in the details, including name and the suburb fields, and six Whitehouse's appeared. He scrolled down to the entry confirming the address he had and a second screen opened.

His gut tightened. A second mortgage had been taken out on the property three months earlier. For a hundred and fifty thousand dollars. Apparently for renovations and an extension.

The smell of the hunt took over, and his pulse quickened.

He grinned, pleased to be acting. It was the process, the chase that motivated him, the results satisfying, he enjoyed the search for the truth and cutting through the social veneer to find human motivations hidden beneath the tangled web of appearances.

He minimised the screen and clicked on a second program, Finance Tracker. This program could log keystrokes and provide more details on financial transactions. To activate the keystroke logger software, he'd need to install it on Whitehouse's pc or laptop. He entered in Jarrod's address, date of birth, and phone number.

A smaller window appeared with a circle spinning agonisingly slowly.

The message 'Processing your request' blinked on

the screen.

A ping went off. A real life one, detectable by his ears, as opposed to the internal pinging. He'd learned over time to reserve his judgement, until the facts became clear. He didn't have the full picture yet, but he would. He opened the second drawer of the dark wooden cabinet to his left, sliding out his notebook, which he used during investigations.

Biting his lip, he had just put pen to paper when the phone chirped on his desk. The small rectangular display showed Ryan's direct line. He picked it up.

"Ryan?"

"Yeah, mate, another investigation? This is becoming a habit. Maybe you should come back into the fold for good."

Connor paused, formulating an appropriate response. He didn't have one. His son-in-law brought up the issue repeatedly at various family events, but Connor had remained evasive, answering questions with another question. Ryan, of course, hadn't fallen for it, and the last few weeks he'd got more persistent. Connor didn't want to tell Ryan that he had considered coming back, but somehow returning felt like a sell-out. He didn't want to go back with his tail between his legs. He knew that popular opinion within the department made him a gold digger, chasing the corporate money private investigation could offer. Pricks like Commissioner Reynolds were the reason he ran for the hills originally, that and Gypsy's close call. Over time, though, the oil of regret had sunk into his pores and memories tugged at him. Sharing a drink with the boys after work, the rush of adrenalin when he solved a case, but mainly the work itself. Three years after his resignation, he could admit that a private investigators life wasn't all it was cracked up to be. The grass, of course, was always greener on the other side.

Not to mention, if Lauren Whitehouse ended up kidnapped or worse, as a private investigator, he'd be denied entry to the crime scene.

"Well, I might for this case," Connor said, "although hindsight's a wonderful thing. Hopefully the Coroner won't be needed on this one."

"Jarrod Whitehouse? A murderer? Hmm..."

"I wouldn't say that. I haven't followed this down. There's a few strings I need to pull. I'll see where it takes me."

"Well, he's been in missing persons for the last four months. He asked for a transfer from CID."

"Why would a senior sergeant with forty years' experience working in a department most cops dream of, ask for a transfer to an outpost like missing persons' months before retirement?"

"A quiet life?" Ryan said.

Connor's lips thinned. "Don't know about that. Seems a bit coincidental that his wife went missing how long after his transfer to missing persons?"

"Four months."

Connor made notes.

"Thanks, Ryan. Anything else I should know?"

"Yeah, he's been on stress leave for the last week."

"Okay. It might be time to visit Jarrod Whitehouse, stressed or not."

"Go easy, Connor."

"Always, mate" Connor said, and he frowned as he put the phone down

He moved his attention back to the computer to continue the initial online enquiries. The screen told him that Jarrod had a computer at home. Unfortunately, it wouldn't list keystrokes logged in the past, including any online searches or websites visited, but maybe, now that he'd established a digital connection by searching for and finding the Whitehouse internet protocol address, he could get the key logger software onto the Whitehouse computers.

Connor picked the pen back up and began a time line. First, the date Lauren went missing, five days earlier. Today's date, the day her sister Elizabeth came to visit him and the investigation began. Four months earlier, when Jarrod transferred from CID to missing persons, and the date the money was withdrawn, the $150K.

He gazed down at his handwritten notes in the notebook, a series of straight lines and notes. So far, Jarrod had asked for a transfer, and then refinanced his home. Connor had a question mark for the possibility of Lauren having an affair. Then Lauren's call to her sister, followed by Elizabeth's follow up visit after Lauren's disappearance.

Staring at the piece of paper, nothing came to him, which was unusual. But he had begun. His gaze wandered to the second piece of paper on the desk, ready to be placed into a case file. An address for the Whitehouse family, 67 Orange Circuit, Montrose. The drive would probably take about an hour and a half each way from inner city Brunswick.

Connor grabbed his wallet and keys from the desk drawer, then stood and turned off all the office lights. He went to the bathroom, and then headed down the hall to talk to Gypsy. She sat more upright this time at the dining table, her hair across her shoulders.

"I'm off to visit Jarrod Whitehouse. He's in Montrose. It's three hours there and back, should see you around three."

She gave him a faint smile. "Want me to come with you?"

"Not this time, but maybe for my next visit. I like having you with me, believe it or not."

She pushed herself up from the chair, walked over to him, and rested her hands on his chest. She gave him a soft kiss. Maybe they were having a moment, after all.

"See you later," he said and headed out the front door toward Black Betty, his beautiful girl, a black, hotted up 1970s Charger. He'd bought the muscle car back when money proved plentiful thanks to the insurance contact.

He threw his wallet and notepad on the passenger seat and started up Black Betty. Her engine throbbed and growled, and he thanked whoever was up there for the chance to keep her.

Since the contract work had been paused, Gypsy had suggested selling Black Betty, to which he'd replied that no one would sell his girl to pay the bills.

Black Betty, produced in the 70s in Australia as part of the VH Valiant series, was a two-door coupe and he loved her, the feel of her cruising across the smooth road, gripping the road like a sleek and powerful panther.

He'd have plenty of time to enjoy Black Betty and chew things over in his mind during the ninety-minute drive.

He reversed out of the driveway and considered his route. He'd probably have around fifteen minutes of driving in congested Brunswick traffic before he hit the freeway. It would be a straight run on the Eastlink freeway for roughly twenty minutes before another longer drive, but in the leafy outer eastern suburbs before he reached Montrose, overall a pleasant drive.

As he drove, the tendrils of two streams of thought mingled and merged in his mind. His marriage, and the investigation into the disappearance of Lauren Whitehouse. The two subjects weren't related, but pressed on his mind with a similar degree of force. There wasn't a specific point at which his relationship with Gypsy had gone from the spark of excitement at being together to the acceptance of the domestic grind, but more a slow erosion. He wondered how to fix it. Maybe he could cook a dinner one night after Mark went to bed, with candles, flowers, and the whole bit. He smiled as he imagined the look of delight on Gypsy's beautiful face. He knew they needed to take more time out to just be together but the treadmill of life had begun just after Mark's birth which had proved overwhelming for both of them. Once the rush of adrenaline wore off, the stress pushed down on him more than ever, an almost physical force.

So, of course he was worried about pissing clients off. He was the bread winner, and they needed to pay bills. Sure, Gypsy helped, and earned quite a bit, but they had a hell of a lot of bills to pay, too.

He now knew what being backed into a corner felt like. He still loved his wife, no question, but wondered if he'd need to make some grand gesture to restore equilibrium to his marriage and bring back the spark. He'd send his sister-in-law a text message, see if Leah would babysit so he and Gypsy could have a night alone together.

As far as the Whitehouse case went, he wondered if his focus on it was due to it being a potentially criminal case, a taste of his former life. With more than a decade as a cop, most people probably figured he was tougher than your average person. Although at times he wondered if tough could be debated, depending on which way the wind blew, waves of pride occasionally washed over him. He'd stuck it out with Victoria Police for a hell of a long time.

The routines and investigatory work comforted him in a way that he knew might seem strange. In times of trouble, he fell back on it like a hammock. It was a hell of a lot easier than domestic life and the pressure of bills and relationships. He'd driven automatically without too much effort before he reached the freeway exit and the reverie left him, snapping him back to reality. The in-car satellite navigation told him he'd be at the home of what remained of the Whitehouse family soon. He wondered if Jarrod Whitehouse would talk to him, most cops knew that investigators were in it for the money, and were if not the enemy, then barely tolerated. Cops were usually too busy to talk to sell outs.

Connor decided he'd begin by asking about Jarrod's work, hoping he'd reveal the reason he asked for a transfer to missing persons. He figured that Senior Sergeant Whitehouse wouldn't need much prompting to complain about his wife going missing, possibly still believing her to be alive if he were innocent. If he'd had a hand in Lauren's disappearance, he would probably moan about something or someone else while revealing pertinent details without realising it. That's what the guilty usually did.

He pulled up at a red light. Orange Circuit was the second on the left. The light went green, and he eased off the brake, scanning the left side of the three-lane main road in search of the street Jarrod Whitehouse lived on. It sounded affluent, but the neighbourhood itself looked like a regular middle class suburb.

The blue line on the sat nav showed him the house was close to the main road, even if Orange was a short U-shaped Circuit. He slowed, as the sterile voice of the sat nav informed him his destination was on the left. He pulled up in front of a white wooden weatherboard home, with window frames painted a dark green. The garden looked loved, the dainty white roses bordering the lawn well pruned and flowering. The grass had been recently mowed.

He turned off the ignition and got out of the car. The sun had disappeared, taking the warmth out of the air, replaced with a piercing blanket of light, with long shards streaming down from grey clouds. He walked down the concrete driveway which ran to the left of the home and stepped across a path of eight circular concrete circles toward a matching green wooden porch.

The old fashioned white door held a window on its top third, with tiny indentations carved into it, possibly to prevent curious visitors peering through. Connor rang the old-fashioned bell by moving the string to and fro, where a ball bearing clanged on the inside of a rusted bell.

He waited, alert to the sound of movement inside. He couldn't make out any sounds, not even a television running.

He turned toward the garden, gazing at it again before scanning the driveway. No car. Maybe it was parked away safely in the lock up garage.

He turned back toward the door. With a click, the door slid open with a quiet creak. Then there was what he could only assume was the rather imposing figure of Jarrod Whitehouse in the doorway.

Bright blue eyes and grey stubble across a double chin combined with short wavy salt and pepper hair gave Connor the impression he was being pierced rather than looked at. The lines around the man's eyes looked more like the circles of bark within a tree trunk than wrinkles. He wore a white t-shirt with a faded grey design on it, untucked from his jeans probably to accommodate the sagging gut hanging over them.

Connor stood up straighter. "Jarrod Whitehouse?"

"Who's asking?"

Connor fished in his pocket for his PI license, tucked inside a leather holder along with his driver's license and business cards. "Connor Reardon. Private Investigator and ex CID."

"Oh, yeah."

"Can I come inside?"

"To talk about what?" Whitehouse left the front door open, but stepped through the outer fly screen door onto the porch to face him.

"Your wife, Lauren."

"Not a good time."

I bet it isn't, but the question is why.

"I'm sorry, I know this is a very difficult time. I've been engaged to find Laura."

"By who? Let me guess my outlaws think I

knocked her off, right?"

It was only once Connor looked Whitehouse in the face at close range on the front porch, with natural light dominating that he realised Jarrod suffered. The toll of losing a wife and potentially bringing up a daughter alone had hit him hard.

"I don't intend to hassle you, but if we can talk inside, maybe between us we can get to the truth."

Whitehouse hung his head and stared at the dried gum leaves skimming across the wooden porch floor. Connor wondered if he'd let him in. He hadn't exactly told him that his sister-in-law, Elizabeth Metcalfe, had engaged his services.

"I already know the truth." Whitehouse shuffled his feet before meeting his gaze. "All right but not long. Five minutes."

He pulled open the fly screen door and held it open for Connor, who followed behind. The floor of honey brown wood ran the length of the hallway. Most of the doors leading off it were closed. Whitehouse eventually slowed down at the end of the hallway where he gestured toward a couch of indeterminate colour and texture, due to the wash of multi-coloured rugs strewn across it. Connor sat and waited until Jarrod composed himself. It took almost a minute before Whitehouse met his gaze again.

"What filth have you heard from Liz, then? Other than me killing off my wife, leaving my daughter without a mother, what else have I supposedly done?" Sun streamed through a window and Whitehouse squinted before propping his left ankle across his right knee.

"I'm actually trying to find Laura, so any information you have about her movements before she left would help." Connor told himself it wasn't a lie, and putting Jarrod's back up would get him nowhere.

Whitehouse turned his head and pushed out a sharp flow of breath. "I wondered if something was up a couple of months ago, but I don't know, as usual, I was distracted by work. She made more of an effort with her looks, new hair, new nails, the whole thing. Usually she wasn't so worried, but three months before she left, I noticed it."

"Did you ask her about it?"

"What, if she was having an affair? No, I didn't." Whitehouse frowned. "At first, I was relieved she'd turned a corner. We'd been at each other's throats, and I'd had enough. We talked about separating, then suddenly she changed. I was relieved the fighting stopped. She started going out more, at first to visit friends, then she couldn't tell me who the friends were, now this..."

"Any ideas who she may have left with?"

"I'd love to know." Whitehouse spoke through gritted teeth. "Her phone's not answering, goes straight to voice mail. Some of her clothes are gone. Her handbag, wallet, and phone are gone."

"Is that her car outside?"

"Yeah. She didn't take it, which is weird." The older man rubbed at his chin.

Connor wondered if the slight tremor in Whitehouse's fingers indicated nerves or grief.

"It does seem unusual." He could ask about the daughter later in the conversation, if Jarrod let his guard down. "You didn't report her as missing?"

Jarrod's jowls wobbled as he pushed himself up from a reclining position in the chair. "Listen, you don't know what it's been like. Do you have kids?"

"I do, a son," Connor said quietly.

He wondered if the detonated fuse on Jarrod's volatile emotional state would explode or simply subside.

"How the hell do you think it feels to tell a ten-year-old girl that Mummy's left and you don't know when she's coming back?" His shoulders curled, and he brought a shaking hand to his forehead. "I've stayed strong. How I'm doing isn't important compared to a little girl's tears."

"I can't imagine what that's like." Connor sat forward on the edge of the couch, resting his forearm on his knee.

Whitehouse rubbed his hand across his face. "She's staying with her grandma for a couple of days, just while I get things together a bit..."

"You didn't report your wife as missing?"

"Oh, for Christ's sake!" The couch creaked as Jarrod jumped up and began pacing, breathing noisily. "How would you do if your wife left you?"

Connor wondered if Elizabeth Metcalfe had reported her sister as missing officially, and if so, if Jarrod had been notified. Connor crossed his arms. "I don't know how I'd go, but I do know this. You either talk to a private investigator, or you talk to police once a missing person's report is filed. I know which I'd prefer."

Jarrod Whitehouse stopped pacing and turned to glare at Connor, hands on his hips and chin thrust out. "Piss off! Get out of my house!"

Blood boiled in his face, the veins in his neck pronounced. He pointed, his right arm ramrod straight, down the hallway toward the front door.

Connor stood up. "Like I said, I'm interested in the truth, wherever that takes me. At some point, you will need to explain the hundred and fifty thousand refinance. Did Laura know about that?"

Jarrod took a step forward. "Get out of my home now, Get out!"

Globules of spittle perched on his lips and chin.

Connor turned and walked down the hallway, shoes clicking on the bone-dry polished floorboards. Jarrod Whitehouse continued ranting from the lounge room.

Connor turned the latch on the front door, opening it quietly, and stared down the hallway before he closed it behind him. Whitehouse was in a fit of rage, purple mottled face and bulging veins.

Shit.

Connor pulled the door closed. Time to get out of there and follow up the next lead.

\#

CHAPTER 4

Connor hadn't had a chance to ask why Whitehouse requested a transfer from CID to Missing Persons. The man was a powder keg, and he'd just lit the fuse.

On the drive home, Connor wondered what he could have done and said differently. Most likely nothing. Jarrod Whitehouse had lost a wife. His emotions were frayed and ready to explode, a barrel of fireworks waiting to be lit. Either he didn't want to talk about his wife leaving him for another bloke, or he really did have a shit load of baggage he couldn't or wouldn't face.

On the drive home, Connor frowned at the road and considered his options. He could call Elizabeth and ask more questions, which might open new possibilities, or dig further into the Whitehouse family's financial affairs, or hunt down clues to Laura's secret lover, if one existed. Possibly at her workplace.

As most detectives knew, the obvious path was

usually the most fruitful one. Money, lust, jealousy, power, and vengeance could turn a seemingly regular person into a raging lunatic, capable of serious injury and in some cases, murder. He just needed to find the frayed thread, the point at which Jarrod and Lauren's seemingly stable middle class lives had unravelled.

He'd revisit the time track of events and assess from there.

He wanted to talk to Gypsy, to hold her. During intense, complex investigations, she'd always been a stable presence. He couldn't wait to see her.

Maybe Leah Gypsy's sister could look after Mark, and he and Gypsy could have a night out together, dinner or a movie. Maybe both.

He slowed the car and pulled into his lane, which thankfully wasn't jam packed with vehicles parked along both sides of the narrow street due to being an inner-city street with narrow houses squeezed together. Not today though. Sighing and running hands through his hair, He got out and locked the car.

As he walked along the short footpath to the front steps, Gypsy opened the fly screen door.

She murmured, "There's a guy waiting for you in the street."

She let the door close behind her, and footsteps faded away as she stepped back inside.

Connor climbed up the steps and reached for the front screen door.

The blow to the back of his head came without warning. He let go of the door, and the world spun. Gypsy screamed his name from inside the hallway. His head hurt like hell, and his eyes flickered closed. He pushed against the desire to fall and failed. The world faded to grey, and he pushed against the greyness to stay in the present. He thrust out his hands which broke his fall as he landed on the concrete porch. He struggled against the hazy wash of unconsciousness. He knew if he succumbed to blackness the enemy behind would either beat him to a pulp or kill him.

A kneecap jammed into Connor's spine. Connor tilted his body to the right. The knee on top of him compensated by shifting its weight to the left. Connor pushed up with his hands and rolled back his right shoulder. The weight of the faceless man rolled off his back.

In the split second that the dark-haired mass of arms and legs attempted to get up, Connor was over him. He thrust his forearm around the man's throat. He squeezed and a gurgle emerged from the man's mouth, along with a cascade of spittle. Gritting his teeth, Connor pulled upward and dragged the man to his feet.

Adrenaline surging, Connor rammed the man's head into his office window at full force. He gritted his teeth as the glass shattered. The man groaned, his head bleeding. His arms still around the man's throat, Connor twisted his body and smashed the stranger's head against the window ledge. The body went limp. He let it fall to the ground.

Out of breath, Connor leaned forward, his hands on his thighs.

Gypsy was out and down the front steps, "Oh, my god, who the hell is that?"

Connor couldn't speak, still out of breath and struggling to process what in the hell had just happened. He straightened up and turned to look at her.

With each palm resting on either side of his face, her eyes scrutinised him. "I've called the police.""

"I need to get him in cable ties. Once he wakes up, he'll come at me again, and this time he'll kill me."

"We need to get you to a doctor"

"Get some cable ties before he wakes up."

"Connor..."

"Just get them, will you? Now. We can't just leave him here" He felt the blood pulsing in a vein on his right temple.

The bleeding man had a full head of dark hair, and despite the blood, Connor at that moment, recognised his enemy for the first time. Joe Reeves, the husband of client Mrs. Helen Reeves, whom he'd recently uncovered as embarking on an experiment with bisexuality.

They'd possibly had a fight and despite his initial thought that Mrs. Reeves wouldn't bring up her husband's betrayal, it must have come out during an argument.

Shit. Joe Reeves didn't move, still unconscious, but Connor didn't want to take any chances. Gypsy came back out and hurried down the steps with cable ties in her hands. She passed them to him without a word, her hair shielding her face.

Squatting beside Reeves, Connor passed the cable ties around the unconscious man's wrists. Reeves' body rocked slightly as Connor tightened the cable ties. The nosy neighbours would love this. Squatting again, Connor pushed two fingers into Reeves' neck, alive although not kicking, thank god. A marked police car arrived, and Connor stood.

The slam of car doors punctured the quiet of the

suburban street. Two uniforms entered the driveway, with matching serious expressions. He didn't recognise them, but they were fully kitted up, both men, both dark haired but one tall and slimmer, the other shorter and well-built.

They stopped a foot away from him, the taller one just behind the stockier one.

Connor decided not to shake hands.

"Connor Reardon. Ex CID, private investigator." He gestured with his head toward Reeves lying below the window, sprawled across the concrete. "You might need an ambulance."

The taller uniform grabbed a walkie talkie from his belt and started talking into it, turning away from them and taking a step or two back down the driveway.

"Senior Constable Bowden." The stocky constable Bowden gestured toward the taller man walking down the driveway. "And he's Constable Newton. What happened here?"

Bowden retrieved a retrieved a battered notebook from his fluorescent vests.

Connor rubbed at the back of his head. Rather than diminishing with time, the pain throbbed harder.

"I arrived back about twenty minutes ago. As I walked up the steps to the porch, he punched me from behind, in the back of the head. He got me down on—"

"You should get the ambulance people to have a look at you," Gypsy said. "That punch in the head—"

"Let me finish," Connor said, not looking at Gypsy. He didn't care if he bit out the words. Maybe it was meant to be reassuring, that she cared about his welfare, but right now she'd completely pissed him off. Why didn't she just get the cuffs when he asked her to?

"He got me down on the concrete, knee in my back. I got him off by rolling my shoulders I got him in a headlock, and his head went through the window. His head hit the window ledge on the way down." Connor rubbed at his temple.

Senior Constable Bowden scribbled in his notebook.

"I see." He barely looked up at them. "Do you know him? Why did he attack you?"

All three of them turned as the flashing lights of the ambulance caught their attention. Constable Newton waved the ambulance into the narrow driveway. As the ambulance stopped, Bowden joined them near the front step. Two paramedics jumped out of the van and jogged across to the prone Joe Reeves, now starting to move his limbs where he lay on the concrete, his words slurred.

A red-haired paramedic in green overalls with high visibility lettering across his back dropped a kit bag on the concrete and kneeled beside the unconscious Joe Reeves. The paramedic put an oxygen mask over Reeves' mouth and began checking vital signs.

"There's a bit of blood and glass on his face. He hit the window?" the red-haired paramedic said.

"Yes," Connor said.

"How long has he been unconscious?" the shorter, darker haired paramedic stood straight, frowning.

"Not long, maybe five minutes. You got here quickly. I think my partner called during the fight so..." Connor turned back to Senior Constable

Bowden. The pounding in his head beat heavier and harder, and he wondered if he'd keel over from the dizziness. "I think I need to sit down."

He took a few tentative steps back toward the front steps and sat on the concrete. Everything swam for a couple of seconds, before the world righted itself.

Gypsy stood in front of him. "Connor?"

He raised his head.

Her face was paler than usual, the dark circles more pronounced. "I'll ask one of the paramedics to come over."

Bringing a hand to his head, he nodded slightly.

The two paramedics had managed to get Joe Reeves onto a stretcher. The two police officers remained standing in front of him as he sat on the front step.

"Can you tell us what happened?" said Newton, not realising the questioning had already begun.

"Yeah," Connor said. "Can we go inside?"

Constable Bowden spoke first. "Why don't you go inside, and we'll have a quick chat to the paramedics."

"Okay." Gypsy extended her hand, and he grabbed it.

He looked at her for the first time since the incident had begun.

"Thank you," he mumbled.

"Do you want to put an arm around me, and I'll help you in?" she said quietly.

"No, thanks, I'll get in okay, but my head hurts like hell."

"Can I get you something?" she said, hovering close to Connor's shoulder. He shook his head.

The loud revving of yet another car broke the

momentary silence and they turned. Connor recognised Ryan's black Hyundai, which didn't stop. The car began a three-point turn, before heading back down the street away from them.

Connor dragged himself up the steps, counted the eight steps it took to get to the couch, and fell backwards onto the seat with a groan.

"I'll make you some hot sweet tea," Gypsy said, and then disappeared into the kitchen.

She was probably worried he had gone into shock, and maybe he had. He didn't really care. All he could focus on was the pain, a metal bolt bashing and clanging inside his head, wishing for it to end. As the kettle began to boil, footsteps thudded in the hallway. Constables Newton and Bowden appeared in the lounge room, pausing just inside the living area.

"Can we come in?" Bowden said.

"Take a seat," Connor said, ignoring the shaking in his voice.

Bowden nodded and sat on the couch beside Connor. Newton took the recliner in the left corner. Gypsy brought in Connor's tea, and he grabbed at the mug. The heat burned his fingers and palms, but he didn't pull them away. He sipped the tea, feeling the heat as it moved through his body. He preferred the sensation of drinking sweet tea to the searing pain in his head.

Gypsy sat to his right. The front door creaked, and rasping breath filled the hall. Then the six foot one form of his son-in-law, Senior Constable Ryan Sheehan, in uniform, entered the living area.

"Connor. I heard something happened here. I came when I could." Ryan took a couple of steps in and stood in front of the couch. "What's going on?"

He took in the sight of Gypsy and Senior Constable Bowden on the couch, his gaze pausing on Bowden's name tag, and then Constable Newton, perched on the edge of the recliner.

"Senior Constable Sheehan. You know this gentleman?" Bowden said.

"Yeah, he's my father-in-law," Ryan said. "Can the paramedics check he's okay? He was punched in the head and he's feeling dizzy," Gypsy said.

Ryan put his hands on his hips. "He needs to make a statement while it's fresh in his mind."

"I can't give out too much. Client related, confidential." Connor bit out the words.

Nausea surged, and he wished the pain would stop.

"Have you met the man before " Constable Reardon frowned and looked up from his notebook

"No," Connor said. "I know of him, and have pictures of him but other than that, no, we haven't officially met."

"Were you conducting surveillance of Mr. Reeves?"

"I can't answer that."

Bowden sighed and scribbled in a notepad. There was no chance of seeing what he had written.

"We need to know what happened. We can't investigate without information." Said Newtown, taking a step toward Connor.

Connor took a deep breath. "He punched me in the head from behind."

Connor paused.

"Go on, Mr. Reardon," Bowden said.

"He had me on the ground with his knee in my back. I rolled my shoulders to the left just a bit, and he counterbalanced, and I managed to roll over. I got him in a head lock and put his head through the window, not hard, though. I just wanted him unconscious, I thought he was going to kill me."

"You said earlier his head hit the window ledge on the way down. Did it fall down, or did you push his head onto the ledge?"

Bowden didn't miss much.

"I pushed his head onto the ledge. Remember, this is someone that punched me in the back of the head, unprovoked, on my property. I thought he was going to kill me. I did just enough to knock him out, not kill him."

"I see." Bowden frowned and continued scribbling in his notepad. "Would you like to press charges?"

"Only if he presses charges, as well. I'm guessing he wouldn't want to tell a magistrate why he punched me from behind. His motivations aren't something he wants made public knowledge."

Constable Newton spoke next. "You said you haven't met him, but he is the husband of one of your clients. "

The frequency of the pounding of his head had reduced from every second to every thirty seconds, and the dizziness had disappeared.

He opened his mouth to speak, but Ryan took a step forward.

"Bearing in mind, Connor was attacked unprovoked on his own property."

Bowden frowned, and his muscles tensed. He glared at Senior Constable Ryan Sheehan. "We're aware of that. All we're asking for is the full story. We need full information to assess the situation, confidential or not, as I'm sure you're aware."

"It's okay, Ryan," Connor said, leaning forward on the couch, his forearms on his knees. "He landed on the ground face up, and I recognised him from his photograph. That's all I can say."

The silence hung heavy and palpable.

Ryan looked across at Connor, meeting his stare, before hanging his head, hands perched on his hips.

"I see," Constable Bowden said finally. "So, you believe whatever you did angered Joe Reeves, which is why he attacked you."

Connor pressed his lips together. "Like I said, there's only so much I can tell you." He managed a weak smile, catching Gypsy's eye.

"I still think you should get checked out at hospital," she said, rubbing her hands across her face.

Ryan walked across to perch on the arm of the couch, next to her. "Don't worry, I said I'll take him to a doctor and I will. Promise."

Gypsy grimaced, lips thinning.

Bowden spoke again, pen perched over his notebook. "Can you get permission from your client to provide us with a statement?"

"Yeah, I'll try," Connor said, running his fingers up and through his hair. " I had no idea this would happen. None of us did."

Bowden rose from the seat. "We'll be in touch. We have the basic facts for now. If you have details from your client, that would help. I'll let you know of the status of the gentleman. If you'd like to press charges, you'll need to come into the station."

"I'll reserve my judgment," Connor said.

Ryan and Gypsy stood up.

"Don't get up Connor," she said. "I'll get the file and find their contact details so you can get permission.

"I'll see you out," Ryan said, stepping toward the front door. He allowed both the officers to pass him and watched as the front door clicked closed.

Connor hadn't moved. He couldn't believe what had just happened; he'd almost killed the bloke. He prided himself on curtailing his urges and emotions, and had done so for many years in the force, so why had he succumbed to the desire to knock the crap out of the guy? What had happened to all his years of training and experience?

He wasn't sure if he was ready to attempt getting up yet, even if the pain in his head had diminished. The couch bounced as Ryan sat down beside him.

"I don't think a visit to the doctor would hurt," he said. "You might have concussion."

Connor looked back at Gypsy. Her face, which was pale most of the time, anyway, had gone another shade of deathly white.

"I'll think about it," he said. "I need a shower."

His body, now heavy as lead, wouldn't easily move from the couch. He slowly dragged himself up and tried to get to the bathroom. He focussed on keeping his balance, ignoring the tightness in his chest. As he reached Gypsy at the hallway, he paused and hugged her. He didn't want to let go. She hugged him back and after a few more seconds, he pulled away, his face inches from hers.

"Can we be friends again?" he murmured.

Her eyes were dark and bright

"We always were," she said.

He kissed her. She kissed him back, instead of just allowing her to kiss him, which somehow made her lips softer. He pulled away, and she rubbed his arm.

Ryan called out as Connor headed for the shower. "Let me know if you change your mind about the hospital"

"I won't," he yelled back, increasing his pace slightly.

In the bathroom, Connor turned on the shower, the warm burst of water soothing him before he'd even stepped in.

As he undressed, his thoughts turned to his two most pressing investigations: Helen and Joe Reeves, and Elizabeth Metcalfe looking for her missing sister, Laura. Something niggled at him, some missing piece of the puzzle. Since he'd been a private investigator, he couldn't recall ever being attacked by a client, or a client's relative, although he'd almost lost his life once, and Gypsy had been shot a few years go. Client's had gone off their rocker in anger but being punched in the head in a surprise attack was a first.

He allowed himself a quick look in the mirror and wished he hadn't. Judging by the magnified cracks in his face he'd aged a couple of decades in the last few hours, and his face, smeared with dirt, appeared only marginally better than his now scruffy-dirty blond hair, sticking up in all the wrong places.

He stepped into the shower stall and groaned. The water beat down across his head, heat radiating through him. He moved into the best position for pain relief and stood there for a moment, running the two current investigations through his mind.

He wanted to go back to the written sequence of events. Plus, the photos, the evidence, and the background of Mrs. Reeves prick-of-a-husband needed another going over, in more detail this time.

He didn't want to get out of the shower but

something propelled him to act, the pinging in his mind returning. There was a clue he'd missed. The water was warm and soothed the aches in his back. The longer he remained, the more his thoughts came back to the file. The photographs were beckoning. Some thread, some tenuous link lurked within it.

He turned off the taps, grabbed a towel, and dried himself off quickly. He grabbed his light brown robe off the floor and tied the belt around his waist. He walked as fast as his pounding head could stand, which was a snail speed. In his office, he flicked on the desk lamp, sat down, and reached over for the file.

Opening the file, he ignored the piles of paper cluttering his desk. He flicked through the form at the front of the pile: Mrs. Reeves personal details, and some notes about her situation. Behind that was an invoice with payment details stapled to it, pages of reports in relation to surveillance plans, financial findings, and social media profiles.

The difference in thickness between the photos and the paper meant he accessed the photos quickly among the papers. He pulled out roughly ten photos. He had more on his hard drive but these were the key ones. He focused on the first. His stomach sank. If his instincts proved correct, Lauren was dead, not missing with a strong chance it was Whitehouse, not a secret lover.

Footsteps hit the small flight of stairs directly across from his desk, and he looked up. Ryan walked over to the desk, hovering beside him.

"Watcha doing?" Ryan said.

"Going through the photos from the Joe and Helen Reeves case," Connor said, moving his gaze back to the files.

The ceiling banged lightly above him. Gypsy must be putting Mark to bed for the night.

The smell of something burning alerted Connor, but as neither Ryan nor Gypsy had mentioned it, he wouldn't either. Besides, maybe they'd tell him that the smell of something burning meant he had concussion and should report immediately to the nearest hospital.

He waited for Ryan to bring up the hospital again, and wondered if he'd use the same annoying persuasive tone.

From the corner of his eye, Connor saw that Ryan lingered a few feet from his desk, with a hang dog expression, head down and shifting his weight from one hip to the other. He was going to make him speak, make him nag about getting checked out by a doctor.

"Want a lift to the doctor?" Ryan said.

"Nah," Connor said.

The enlarged colour photo he held in his right hand drew him in. Front and center, two men locked lips in a passionate open mouthed kiss, oblivious to the world. In the background, leaning against a wall, a heavy-set woman smiled. To the untrained eye, she looked like a woman, but the throat, the jaw, and the shoulders gave it away, no matter how thick the pancake make-up. The shoulder length well-set dark brown hair and the immaculately applied make up transformed the man, unrecognisable to most. But Connor knew him. Jarrod Whitehouse.

He squinted at the photograph and his mouth twisted.

"You know Gypsy'll crack the shits if you don't get

checked out," Ryan said.

Connor dropped the photograph. "What's new?"

"This is serious. You could've been killed."

Connor peered up at Ryan. He pushed up from the chair and stood a foot away from him behind the desk. "Yeah, I could've but I wasn't. We know the risks when we take this job on, investigator or cop."

Ryan took a small step closer and lowered his voice. "What's the go?"

"I'm not sure yet, but I think I've found the link between two cases. A link that explains why Joe Reeves did this."

Ryan stared at him. "You going to tell me?"

"I haven't put it all together yet, no proof. When I have, you'll know before anyone else."

Ryan frowned. "Keep safe, mate."

"I always do." Connor allowed himself a wry smile.

Gypsy made her way down the stairs and appeared at the doorway to his office. She rested her hands on either side of the doorway.

"What are you still doing here? I thought you were going to the hospital?" Mouth open, she looked from Connor to Ryan, and then back to Connor.

"Come here," Connor said, his voice low, extending his hand out toward her.

"I'll head off," Ryan said. "I'll give you a call later."

Gypsy walked toward Connor, murmuring a goodbye to Ryan as he squeezed past her. He closed the front door behind him.

She stood across from Connor, beside the office chair where he now had managed to get up to, even if he did prop himself up with fingers splayed across the desk top. "I'm worried about you," Gypsy said. "You probably have a concussion. The blood's gone now but seriously, honey, please go and get checked out. That was scary as hell."

Connor took her hand in his. "I'm sorry I was grumpy with you earlier. I had no idea when he would gain consciousness, and I'm sure when he does wake up, he'll want to kill me. He'll have to join the queue."

"It's okay," she said, locking her gaze on him. "The idea of losing you scares the crap out of me."

He wanted to say, now you understand how I felt every time you took on one of your vengeance cases, your quests for justice, but decided it would be better left unsaid. Besides, he still grappled with what he had almost done to Joe Reeves.

Instead, he looked at Gypsy, really looked at her. Her face had collapsed and sunken into itself

"I shouldn't have asked it of you. To push down your abilities, not use them It wasn't fair and I don't want it to get in the way," Connor said, taking her hand.

"You were under pressure, and I'm almost getting used to your grumpiness. Besides, I should have just got the damn cable ties. You were right, if the guy woke up he, would have killed you."

"I'm not talking about that," he said, staring right at her, hoping she could sense his intention, what he wanted to tell her. Instead, right now, he would just damn well say it. "I mean turning off your abilities, your gift. It's selfish, and I wonder now if it's come between us. It's been years. I'm so sorry."

Her eyes filled. "Oh, god, Connor."

Her chin wobbled, and she reached for him. He held her, and although her back didn't shake and the sobs weren't obvious, her body vibrated in tiny almost unnoticeable shockwaves. He couldn't decide if her ability to suppress her grief, if that's what it was, saddened him more than the knowledge of how much pain he'd caused.

She pulled away from him and wiped wetness from under her eyes. The back of his throat ached.

"I couldn't turn it off, the visions, visits from the dead, messages from spirits. I just didn't I didn't tell you. There's so much between us that I don't say, I can't say. It's killing us." The look of agony in her bright eyes burned him, a hot poker searing through his chest. "I want our marriage to be like it was, back when we supported each other, loved each other. We're bogged down. I don't want to be in a rut anymore."

He brushed the hair out of her eyes, tucking a lock behind her ear. "I've been so focused on getting money in, paying the bills, getting through each day that I couldn't see anything else, including you. I'm so sorry."

Tears spilled out of her eyes, dripping down her cheeks, and she wiped them away quickly.

"The thing is," Gypsy said, "I know you think you're protecting me, by flicking the switch, but it doesn't protect either one of us. Neither one of us used our abilities for the last couple of years, but it didn't stop that bastard from nearly killing you."

Score one for his wife, although she didn't say it to score points. Not acting on their abilities didn't protect them; it left them in the same position, or made them even more vulnerable.

"Life is hard enough as it is, " Gypsy said. The tears had paused. "What we can do is an advantage, a gift. We should use it to help others. It doesn't hurt, despite what happened in the past. No one needs to know what we do but us."

He struggled to find the words to respond.

"Besides," she continued, "I had a vision last night, about your missing woman, I think."

"You did? Where is she?" He took a step toward her, putting his hand on her forearm.

"She's dead, buried in a shallow grave."

\#

CHAPTER 5

Connor leaned away from Gypsy, propping himself up by placing one hand on the wall. Lauren Whitehouse murdered. If he thought telling loved ones about cheating spouses was rough, reporting a murder was worse. He'd done it too many times before, and certainly didn't want to do it again as a private investigator.

His stomach dropped, and the skin on the back of his arms prickled up. "What did you see? The killer?"

"From the back. I didn't see his car or registration either, but considering it was pitch black, I thought I did well. All I saw was him digging the grave and dragging her body into the hole. He took a quick look at everything after he was done, and then drove off."

"Where?"

"That's the problem. I don't recognise the location. I reckon it's somewhere out west, thought. There was a lot of open land, and he buried her in a side road, a dirt track with a few trees around it. There were lights from businesses, but way off in the distance. Other than that, I'm sorry, no idea."

"Shit. I wish she'd run off and disappeared. At least she'd be alive." Connor combed his hair with his fingers and landed back in the office chair.

"Me, too."

"What did the killer look like? I know it was dark in your vision, but did you see the car or killer? "

She dragged a chair closer to Connor and sat down with a sigh. "I wish. I wish I could draw, I could show you the picture. The killer had business clothes on, a royal blue and white striped shirt, a black belt, and dress pants. Dark hair. He looked about five ten. The car, well, it's a sedan, silver coloured. Other than that, no idea. I don't think he's done this before, though."

"Why do you say that?" Connor leaned forward in the chair.

The office had darkened but neither of them moved to turn lights on.

"He was horrified, terrified. It wasn't a thrill kill or done in anger, I think. I reckon spur of the moment or accident."

"Do you know for sure the body is Lauren Whitehouse?"

"No. But why else would I be dreaming about a woman killed? The body he took out of the car looked shortish, though, and not big. He wrapped her up in a pink sheet so I didn't see her face. I'll never forget the finger though, one of her fingertips poking up through the earth. That's how shallow the grave is." She shivered.

"I can check on Lauren's size with her sister. In the meantime, I want to see this picture or vision of yours. Tomorrow morning, I'll get back on investigating. We still have no evidence, and we need it fast." He didn't tell Gypsy that her vision, combined with his recent deduction regarding Whitehouse and the photos in the Reeves case meant he was almost back to square one.

"Yeah, I'm tired too, exhausted, actually. We'll talk tomorrow. Today was hell." She rose from the chair and stood in front of him. "C'mon. Let's go."

She looked at him, a twisted smile in place.

"Okay," Connor said, but he didn't move. His bones ached and the headache had subsided to a dull throb.

"Here's a wild idea. Come to bed, and I'll show you the vision."

Connor looked up at her and pushed himself up, stretching out his back with his hands on his spine. "It's been a while since we did that."

"Yeah, more than three years. The last time it happened was with Isabella. But it could be fun trying." Her tired smile widened.

He took her hand and followed her the short distance from the office to their bedroom. After visiting the bathroom, he took off his clothes and fell into bed, groaning as he did so. She was right; it had been an exhausting day. He wanted to wipe out his internal hard drive and start again, forget the day had happened.

He gazed across at Gypsy taking her clothes off in the lamplight. After several years, he still enjoyed watching her undress. She had no idea how sexy she was, although he'd told her enough times. She tucked in her elbows and turned away from him as usual. At some point, she'd be willing to disrobe in front of him without consideration. She slipped a gray night shirt over her head and slid into bed.

"Ah," she said as she hit the mattress. "I love my bed. I really should turn in earlier each day but..."

He shuffled his body around toward her, lying on his left side. "So, will you show me this vision? Besides the vision that is you, that is."

"Sleazebag," she said but he heard the smile in her voice.

She shuffled across the bed to kiss him, her lips warm and soft. Close up, her eyes magnetised him, her sweet breath tantalising. He moved closer.

"Take my hand," Gypsy murmured.

She pulled her right hand from beneath the pillow and offered it to him. He took the small soft cradle and nestled it into his palm, the bird-like bones of her fingers linked with his.

"Let's go," she whispered.

His mind's eye activated with pictures of nothing other than swirling mist. The mist cleared, giving way to inky darkness. Then he saw it, the lights of a car, dimmed to parkers. Life signs of homes or businesses twinkled on the horizon. The car, a station wagon, pulled up to the deserted spot, an unsealed road and dry dirt and mud crackled as the car pulled to a stop. To the right of the car stood several mature trees, overhanging the road. A man stepped out, his shoes clicking on the asphalt. Connor focused his attention on him, but his face was black, not discernible at all.

Shit

He could make out the murky figures height, around five foot nine inches, and his shirt which appeared to be white and dark stripes. He wore black pants. His dark hair although it matched the cover of dark, shone in the moonlight.

The faceless man lifted the back door of the car. Inside, an uneven rectangle took up most of the space, with one end at a strange angle, wrapped in sheets in the car's trunk. More than likely a dead body.

He was a murderer.

Connor pushed down the surging frustration, which he knew from experience wouldn't help keep it down permanently, only long enough to stay out of trouble. The murderer dragged the body out of the car, grunting and heaving. It hit the dirt with a sickening thud. He struggled to drag it a few metres, until he reached a tree next to a dilapidated fence. He stood with hands on hips, gasping until his breath returned to normal.

After about thirty seconds, he walked back to the car and reached inside to retrieve a shovel. The shovel scraped along the dirt as the murderer walked back to a spot just beside the wrapped body and began digging.

Waves of terror, horror, and desperation rolled off the faceless murderer, a tangled web of heightened emotions. Maybe he suffered remorse, but none of it reduced Connor's rising fury.

As the murderer dug the hole, Connor surveyed the horizon, hoping to latch onto a landmark, maybe a business or a large building. In the pitch dark, he thought he saw a three storey concrete building, on the far left of the horizon.

The murderer's tousled hair blew in the light breeze. He dropped the shovel, bent over the lifeless form, and began dragging it less than a metre until it fell into the shallow grave. His heavy breathing began again as he gripped the shovel and started filling in the hole. His movements were hurried, panicky.

It took him only a minute or two. He wiped one hand on the other, stood back for a moment to look at his work, and then headed to his car. He threw in the shovel, and then slammed the back of the station wagon closed. A few large fragments of earth dangled from the roots of a tree, threatening to drop to the ocean below.

He got into the drivers' side of the car, started it up, and was gone.

Connor estimated from start to finish the burial of the body took less than half an hour.

The picture faded to black. Gypsy turned onto her side to look at him. Nausea churned in his stomach.

"That was the body of Lauren Whitehouse?" he said.

"Unfortunately, yes, I think so," Gypsy said, her voice hushed.

"God. We need to locate the body and let Ryan know once we find it. I can't tell my client her sister is dead until there's evidence. It might pay to look for landmarks like the square block of a building nearby, maybe somewhere out west"

"How do we do that? It could take forever."

"I know but we need to start somewhere." Connor sat up in bed "Tomorrow, I'm going back to my list of events as they happened. There's a link between the two cases, Whitehouse and Reeves, and I wonder if that's the key."

Gypsy closed her eyes for second before opening them and staring at him, her eyebrows drawing together. "You saw the finger?"

"What finger?" A prickling sensation crawled up the back of his arms.

"When the bastard buried the body in the shallow grave, he left a finger sticking up above the ground. In his hurry to get out of there, he must not have seen it, but I did."

Connor swallowed hard and fell back onto the mattress. "Bastard. Someone will find the body soon. A dog or a jogger. We need to trace that car somehow. We'll see if we can track the location ourselves, otherwise we'll have to wait for the media to tell us."

"Do we call Ryan?"

"Not unless we have some scrap of info to give he can act on. He can't tell me anything about cases or police business. He'll put his job in danger if he does, but I can feed info to him. I might call him in the next day or so when I have more hard stuff, but right now, it's' circumstantial and theories. He'll need more than that to get a warrant or question anyone."

Gypsy sighed. "It's horrible to think about, that mother being murdered, but I do like working with you on a case. Reminds me of the good old days."

She smiled faintly.

He reached forward and caressed her cheek, and then glided his hand upwards to stroke her hair. "The good old days. Yeah. I like being friends."

She leaned closer and kissed him softly. He grabbed her by the waist, guiding her to him. These were the moments he remembered, the ones that pushed the black shit, the clanging memories to the back of his mind where they faded into oblivion.

That was exactly what he planned on doing tonight. Enjoying Gypsy in the here and now and

forgetting about the darkness, even just for one night.
###

CHAPTER 6

Something niggled at the back of Connor's mind. He knew the being from somewhere but her name escaped him. Electricity raced up his back and neck. The floating sensation hid behind his desire to understand what was happening and who stood in front of him in what looked to be a dark, inky nothingness. The pitch blackness behind her swirled and seethed. Her blonde hair hug oily, stringy, unwashed. She stared at him unflinching, rubbing at her stomach lovingly, looking down at it.

Was this Lauren Whitehouse speaking from the grave?

He wondered if she would talk to him and continue staring at him indefinitely. He turned and scanned his surroundings to get an idea of where he was, but strangely he couldn't make out a single object, no tree, leaf, or building.

As she extended her hand to him, reaching out to take his, realisation struck him. The woman before him was Lauren Whitehouse. She wanted to get in touch, and this dream, if it was a dream, was how she intended to do it.

"Who killed you? Why?" he said.

Wouldn't she tell him? Lauren Whitehouse, however, simply frowned and shook her head.

Why wouldn't she speak? Maybe she couldn't speak; maybe she wanted to tell him but couldn't. Did that mean she was dead? If that was the case, common sense dictated she'd give him the information he desperately needed, closure for the family, a clue to the killer's identity and for Lauren herself. Something.

"Who did this? Did someone hurt you?" he continued. She couldn't ignore him forever.

However, she simply smiled and shook her head, this time placing one hand on her heart.

What was the significance of the gesture? Love? Something else? Was she trying to tell him that her husband did this?

He opened his eyes and she was gone. He lifted his hand to his neck, which felt stiff and sore. His skin was warm to the touch.

Pushing back the covers, he headed for the shower. Maybe it had been simply a dream, his subconscious playing tricks on him. After years of not using his abilities, not receiving messages from the living, or intercepting communication meant between psychics, was Lauren Whitehouse determined enough to break through the mass of spiritual buffer to deaden the signals, had she broke through?

Maybe it was a coincidence, after all, he had just gained Lauren as a client. He wondered why he kept doubting himself, frustrating himself now. Maybe if he went with it, he would get more clients, and solve more crimes, and yeah, maybe clients saw it as a plus point. Or maybe she was trying to tell him it wasn't his fault.

Oh, God.

A claw tugged inside his stomach, pulling its edges into a ball. Gypsy would surely berate him for indulging in self-invalidation but he still had not completely accepted his abilities. The doubt, at times, seemed agonising as it should be. He might have cost this woman her life. He'd almost prefer the physical pain of the day before than this anguish, the constant self-invalidation. Was it or wasn't it a bona fide vision?

He still had the headache from the attack, although it had almost lifted, replaced instead with a mild throb. His heart pounded as he thought about the investigation at hand. He hoped there'd be no more unexpected disasters like yesterday to screw up his plans.

He headed for the kitchen where he found Gypsy in the kitchen cooking breakfast, and Mark propped up in his high chair. He walked over and planted a kiss on her forehead.

"Morning, lovely," he said.

Gypsy frowned at the frypan where a couple of egg yolks had burst. Her perfectionist nature wasn't doing her any favours.

"Morning." She didn't or wouldn't look at him. "Have you ever wondered if our abilities passed down to our son?"

Connor halted halfway to the kitchen table. "What are you talking about? Did you see something?"

"Let's not talk about it now. Maybe after I come back from kindergarten." She rolled her eyes toward

Mark, a signal that she shouldn't talk about it in front of their son.

"Yeah, okay," Connor said, and sat at the table. He looked across at Mark, still in his pyjamas.

"Hi, gorgeous," Connor said, with a smile.

"Da-da," Mark said, eyes bright and mouth wet.

Connor reached across to brush his cheek. "I love you, son. You know that, you bundle of cuteness?"

"Da-da," Mark said again, raising his hands as he did so.

Gypsy brought the platter of eggs and bacon across to the table. Damn it smelled good.

"This is nice," Connor said. "Thanks."

She smiled. "It happened this morning. I heard Mark babbling upstairs in his room and realised he was awake." They both looked at Mark who still had his hands in the air.

"Pway," Mark said, still smiling.

"Yes, honey, we'll play later," Gypsy said, taking a bite of her bacon.

"What's on the agenda for you today, lovely?" Connor stabbed his fork into a piece of fried potato.

"Actually, only few hours today. I've almost caught up on my writing so I might lash out and do some admin."

"I might be out on the road today, depending on what comes up this morning. Want to go for a ride?"

"Yeah, I'd like to get out of the house for a while," she said, finishing off the last of her eggs.

"Well, I'm just taking a quick look at something before we leave " Connor said, pushing up from the table.

He headed toward his office. His thoughts turned to the investigation. What did he have so far?

A mother and sister missing, possibly murdered. A grieving husband, a senior sergeant moved to a new department coincidentally just four months from retirement. Large sums of money landing in his account for a supposed home renovation. An unfaithful husband, a possible closet bisexual, who didn't want his wife to know about his other life, but his secret had been revealed.

The link between the two cases?

Blackmail.

He knew that once he followed the money, it would lead to the worm who had killed Lauren Whitehouse. He wouldn't give up, not a chance in hell. He walked back to the office with a renewed sense of purpose and determination surging in his chest.

He slid into his chair, making himself comfortable. He took the file from its place at the top of the pile perched on the corner of his desk and opened it. He flicked through the pages until he found the time line of events he started just two days earlier.

He had:

November 12th – Jarrod Whitehouse requests move to Missing Persons Unit – Date for retirement from police force set at 1st March

December 3rd – Jarrod and Lauren Whitehouse take out a loan against their home for $150,000 with the purpose of renovations

Thursday 11th Feb – Lauren calls her sister Elizabeth distraught asking if she and her daughter Juliette can stay with her for a while – trouble in the marriage?

Saturday 13th Feb – Elizabeth visits Lauren. Car in driveway but Lauren nowhere to be seen.

Sunday 14th Feb – Elizabeth calls Connor distraught, suspecting Jarrod, her brother-in-law, has killed her sister.

Monday 15th Feb – Elizabeth visits Connor promising to report her sister as missing with police.

Connor rubbed at his lips, pen poised over the paper. He became aware of Gypsy hovering at the top of the three steps facing his desk. Mark wriggled in her arms.

"We just wanted to say goodbye." She smiled faintly.

Mark extended his chubby sausage arms, encased in a Spiderman t-shirt. Connor pushed off from his chair and headed over to them, Mark's dark pools of eyes matching Gypsy's.

Buds of heat crinkled in his chest. He put one arm around Gypsy's shoulder and kissed her softly. Mark stretched his neck to look up at them both, and brought his hand up to Connor's cheek, resting it there.

This was what life was all about. The soft gentleness of his two-year-old son's palm rubbing on his cheek, staring into his eyes. Mark had the soft look a child yet also a piercing gaze of wisdom, one that had seen and heard many things, good and bad. As Connor held his son in his gaze, he vowed that nothing or no one would ever come between him and his family.

"Bye, lovely," he said to Gypsy, "and thank you."

"For what?" she said.

He didn't care if she was fishing for a compliment. He'd give her what she wanted or needed to hear.

"For this. For you, for my son. Thank you." His voice sounded more hoarse than usual to his own ears.

Gypsy bowed her head and hoisted Mark's kinder bag further up her shoulder but not before her eyes misted over.

"Let's talk when I get back huh? About that thing..."

"I remember." He said. "I might need your help if I can, too."

"Sure," she said and headed outside.

Connor scuttled back into his chair, eager to carry on where he left off.

He began writing questions on the page below the timeline of Lauren's disappearance.

1.   Why didn't she take her car with her?

2.   Why didn't her husband or her sister report her as missing immediately?

3.   What happened to the $150,000 loan?

4.   If she has been murdered, where is the body?

Connor decided to focus on the money trail first as potentially offering more answers. He reached across the desk to activate the mouse and fire up the investigatory software. He'd installed it around the time he acquired a lucrative contact with an insurance company investigating the validity of various claims, and the tailor-made software had proved unfailingly useful.

His first stop was to find out where the $150K went. He tapped in the details for Jarrod Whitehouse. The bank account was a joint one in both Lauren and Jarrod's name, and thankfully hadn't yet been frozen. Funds landed in the bank account December 19th. He clicked on a new search, setting the filter for outgoing payments of ten thousand dollars or more leaving the account.

The egg timer invaded the screen for around ten seconds as the software performed a search. Connor sat up straight in his chair, pulling it closer to the desk as the program pinged to notify him of search results.

At least six payments had been made, the first for twelve thousand dollars, the second for fourteen thousand, and then increasing in both amount and frequency. In total close to ninety thousand dollars had been paid by Lauren and Jarrod Whitehouse to Paradise Bay investments, the last payment for twenty-two thousand made just a week prior to her disappearance. The date of the first payment was January 12th, and the last payment on February 14th, the same day Elizabeth Metcalfe visited Connor.

All eight payments were to the same recipient: Paradise Bay Trust Investments Pty Ltd.

Interesting.

Connor minimised the financial search software and clicked to open the online search engine. He searched for Paradise Bay Trust. Nothing.

His next stop was the ASIC website, Australian Securities and Investment Commission. All trusts and companies needed to list their details with the governing body. He typed in Paradise Bay Investments Pty Ltd in the search field. Within seconds, results appeared.

Hugh Fraser owned Paradise Bay Investments.

The name sounded familiar. Hugh Fraser was either a public figure or had been mentioned in the media. Connor's fingers almost became tangled amongst themselves in the excitement of tapping the keys; the thrill of the hunt was real whether it occurred in a dark suburban street, the hills and valleys of various rural areas, or an online search for perpetrators of fraud, blackmail, and possibly murder.

His heart thudded a little faster, knocking against his ribcage.

He paused, frozen in position, as he read the media article from eight months prior.

Hugh Fraser, you dirty dog.

Hugh, in a former life, had been a property developer, and for a while, he'd ridden the wave. He invested in multiple developments of units and apartment blocks worth hundreds of millions of dollars. He bought the land cheap and stacked tiny units on it, modern and faceless, each one exactly like the other.

They'd sold off the plan in record time, young urban professionals flocking to Hugh's company, Elite and Beyond Property Group. The cashed up and trendy buyers had been lured by loopholes in tax law, negative gearing the properties as investments and hoped to reap the rewards.

However, twelve months ago, Hugh's greed had driven him to new extremes. He'd sold 60 apartments and due to a dispute with the builder, the properties had never got off the ground, quite literally.

Numerous creditors, including sub-contractors led by the high-profile builder, not to mention the many property investors, had lost their dreams. They'd cashed in all they could lured by big promises, and lost thousands of dollars on a deal big on promises and low on follow through.

Hugh had gone into hiding, laying low at his property in Upwey, based at the foot of the Mount Dandenong ranges. Of course, given time, several of his creditors had tracked him down and turned up seeking satisfaction.

One of the builders, Greg Newham, had a gun and wasn't afraid to use it.

Hugh had retreated to his underground cellar, via a trapdoor at the rear of his property. By way of a small and fortuitously placed underground tunnel, he'd followed it through to the end, which emerged at the boundary fence on his property which backed onto a school. As several furious creditors fired at the property they thought he was in at that time, demanding he come out and show himself, Hugh was already in his vehicle and heading for the hills.

Greg Newham was charged, and the matter died a slow death in the media.

Hugh Fraser had filed for bankruptcy a few weeks after the shooting. Of course, several of the more desperate media outlets had found him, chasing him with cameras and mics, but Hugh had simply responded with the perennial fallback position of 'no comment.'

The farce had occurred nearly eleven months earlier.

Six months ago, however, Hugh Fraser had formed a new company, Fraser Family Trust, otherwise referred to as the Paradise Bay Fund.

Interestingly, Jarrod Whitehouse was making regular payments to a disgraced builder's family trust account. The key was to learn whether this money was for renovations which to Connor's untrained eye, hadn't occurred, or whether these were payments to either keeping Hugh Fraser quiet, or were payments for services rendered.

Such as murder for hire.

The quiet hum of the silver seven seater vehicle

increased in volume until Gypsy parked at the end of the driveway, yanking the park brake on.

Connor shifted to look past his computer screen, watching her through the front window as she turned the car off, got out, ran her fingers through her hair, and then activated the electronic lock. She headed up the steps to the front door, purple handbag slung over her shoulders and two coffees in her hand.

She had coffee. The woman got more attractive with every passing minute.

The front door clicked open, and then there she was, standing at the top of the three narrow steps that lead to his office. Her cheeks were flushed and her deep bright eyes adjusted to the light and became aware of his expression, and the opened folder on his desk.

She stepped down and sank into a seat opposite his desk.

"Best part of the day." She smiled and slid one of the coffees across to him.

"Thanks," he said. He paused to take a sip of the coffee, leaning back in his chair before placing the cup in front of his keyboard. "I've made some interesting discoveries while you were away."

"Oh, yeah, like what? We've won the lotto? You're quitting your day job and you've bought tickets to the Bahamas?"

"Not quite," he said. "Most crimes are motivated by greed, lust, jealousy, or money. I decided to follow the money and pulled a few strings to see what was at the end. I found something interesting. I'm just not sure yet exactly what it means."

"Oh, yeah. Where did the yellow brick road lead then?" One of her eyebrows wriggled upwards.

"To Hugh Fraser, a former property developer."

"Hugh Fraser? Where have I heard that name before?"

"Probably in the media. He owed more than half a million bucks to investors for properties they paid for and never got. The builder and some of the creditors tracked him down. The builder fired shots, and Hugh escaped out of a secret underground tunnel."

"Seriously?"

"Yeah, seriously. Greg Newham was charged, and Hugh Fraser went bankrupt. Hugh formed a family trust a few months ago, and Jarrod Whitehouse has been making regular payments into it to the tune of ninety thousand dollars, spread out over six payments."

"Dodgy bastard. Those poor people." She crossed her arms and turned away, lips pressed together until they were almost white.

"Which begs the question. Why did Jarrod Whitehouse pay Hugh that kind of money? According to the bank, he needed 150K for a home renovation but as far as I could see when I visited his home, not a stick has been changed."

"Obviously, he wanted his wife out of the way, and Hugh Fraser knew the right people to get the job done."

"Maybe, that or hush money. Whitehouse had a secret he didn't want anyone to know, especially his wife. The question is how Hugh Fraser found out about it."

"What kind of secret?"

He didn't want to give her too much information, worried she'd do as she had in years gone by and take an investigation and run off on her own with it.

"What's more important right now is that I talk to Ryan. He doesn't work in Missing Persons, but he does work in Criminal Investigations Bureau, and whether this was blackmail or murder, or both, he needs to know about it."

"You can't leave me in suspense like this, Connor. What the hell did Whitehouse do that cost him nearly a hundred grand to keep it quiet?"

"What kind of things would a cop want to keep quiet?"

"I dunno. You'd know better than I do. An affair, drug problem, mental health issues, money problems?"

"Nah, cops run into those problems pretty regularly. This was something out of the box, unusual, not your usual habit."

"How to put an idiot in suspense eh?"

Connor opened his mouth, but was interrupted by the land line ringing loudly on his desk. The call number displayed showed Ryan's mobile number.

"Speak of the devil," Connor said. "It's Ryan. I better take this."

He answered the phone, keeping his tone direct and to the point.

"Thought I'd check in and see what's up," Ryan said. "How's it going?"

"Oh, you mean the headache? All good, almost back to business as usual." Connor rubbed his fingers across his mouth. "Listen, while I've got you on the phone, has the missing person's report on Lauren Whitehouse been filed?"

"You know I can't tell you that." Ryan's voice had reduced dramatically in both pitch and volume. "I'll lose my job."

Connor let out a breath. Gypsy looked at him, the raised eyebrow making an encore performance.

"I know, but you can't blame me for asking. I do have information that will affect the investigation of her disappearance, though. I know it's not your department as such, but when Lauren is found, alive or dead, the information I've discovered could come in useful."

Ryan paused. "Okay, mate, how about you come by after work tonight? I'd swing by your place but Isabella's teething and Christie's practically tearing her hair out. I reckon she'd like to talk to someone other than me."

"Right," Connor said. "I'll ask Gypsy and Mark to come along then. Say around 7.30?"

"Sounds good," Ryan said, and the line went dead.

Gypsy shifted onto the edge of the seat. "What was that all about?"

"Ryan suggested we go over to visit later. Christie could do with a friend right now, and I don't think her father will do the job. Plus, this case is moving at a rapid rate and I can't arrest anyone, but Ryan can."

"Is it really that close?"

"Close enough that he needs to be involved." He rubbed at his chin and pursed his bottom lip. "What were you hinting at this morning? Something up with Mark that I need to know about?"

Gypsy coughed and looked at the floor. "What do you think Mark can do given our abilities?"

"We'll find out I guess. Why?"

"I went up there last night when I heard him babbling away, only I don't think he was babbling to himself. There were beings up there, spirits. I can see them occasionally, transparent figures. When I got to the room, he was sitting up in his cot staring. I saw them too. Mark said 'friends,' and it was clear as day, his pronunciation of it. "

Connor couldn't speak, so Gypsy continued.

"Some of the beings in his room weren't exactly friendly. I lay him back down and rubbed his back and calmed him down a bit. I sent a message to his friends to let them know they should go away and come back later. Some of them did but the rest of them..."

"What are you saying? That he's a psychic, too?"

"I'm saying we should be more aware of this sort of stuff with him. If Mark did inherit our abilities, now is usually the time when it presents itself. And as I left, the door banged closed. These weren't your average spirits, not the friendly type. I'm worried about our son and what this means."

Connor rubbed at the frown etched deeply into the middle of his forehead. "What do you want me to do?"

"You're a Sentinel, so you can break the connection. Nip this in the bud before it escalates."

"Okay, I'll go up there shortly. I'm not keen but for my son, anything."

They looked at each other.

Connor took in a large breath, and then let it out slowly. "Anyway, back to this investigation. I wondered if you wanted to come along with me on this one."

Her cheeks flushed. "Does a cat have a bum? You bet I do, just like the old days."

She shifted her chair closer to the other side of his desk.

"Great. Next on the list is Hugh Fraser's address.

I thought we'd pay him a visit."

"I like it. I'll go grab us some snacks while you ponder " She rose from the chair and left, flicking her hair toward him.

He brought the computer out of sleep mode by waving the mouse across the mouse pad. The financial tracking software was open. It served a dual purpose, not only in providing data on financial transactions but in skip tracing. If Hugh had moved house or left the state, the Subject Locator function should know about it.

He didn't have Hugh's date of birth but from the photograph on the newspaper article, he looked similar although scruffier, around five foot nine with short dark hair. The dark brown hair captured his attention in stark contrast to Hugh's lined face, an obvious dye job.

With a jolt, Connor realised the man who'd dug the body fit Hugh's description. True, neither he nor Gypsy had seen his face, but the man before them could be the murderer. He clicked on the screen which notified him that six results had been found by the IntQuery program for his search on Hugh's name and address. Only one of the Hugh's lived in Upwey. He figured the man may not have experienced much remorse after the sour business dealings but he wouldn't be so bold as to stay in the same property where creditors had taken pot shots at him would he?

He'd soon find out.

He had a rough idea of how he'd get there and the maps function on his mobile phone told him it would take 92 minutes to get from Brunswick to Upwey. Time for a road trip to meet the dodgy dealer himself. "Gotcha, weasel." Connor leaned back in his chair, mouth turning upwards. He rubbed on the stubble across his chin.

Gypsy headed back into the office. "Who you talking to? Me?" she pulled her hand out of a packet of chips, munching on them loudly.

" The pathetic excuse for manhood that did this. I figure he'll be alert for signs someone's onto him, and I'm getting close. "

She sat down, leaning her elbows on his desk. "Where's Hugh Fraser hiding out these days?"

"Upwey, believe it or not. He hasn't moved, or it doesn't look like it. The software has a listing for H Fraser in Upwey, private, of course." He stood up and grabbed his jacket and walked toward the hook in the hallways in search of his keys.

Gypsy stood up. "We're going right now"

"No time like the present."

"Wait, give me five minutes." She raced for the bedroom.

Hugh Fraser may not be home, but he didn't want to take the chance of forewarning the guy that they were coming.

Connor found his wallet, keys, and phone and pressed the button to unlock the car from the hallway.

"Gypsy!" he called behind him, turning his head and then took a step toward the open door.,

A muffled reply filtered out from the bedroom.

Gypsy came running out of the bedroom, zipping up one of her boots, purple bag slung over her shoulder. She sounded out of breath.

"Okay let's go crazy." She suppressed a grin, unsuccessfully.

CHAPTER 7

After an hour drive, Connor and Gypsy stood outside the gate leading to Hugh Fraser's enormous property.

His stomach growled.

"Let me do the talking" said Connor, casting her a sideways glance.

"We'll see," Gypsy said looking down at her shoes.

The large property scrawled across half an acre. In places the sprawling lawn faded to bare earth, in others underneath the large ancient trees moss had taken over. The home itself had been fashioned after a quaint country cottage, with bottle green shutters matching the pitched roof, and the white rendered façade.

Gypsy and Connor shared a look as they stood at a large white wrought iron gate across the driveway. The large gate squeaked as the pushed it open, and small white pebbles crunched underfoot as the made their way down the slight slope of a gravel driveway. As they walked past a white station wagon toward the front door, the driver's door opened. A man stepped out, thin and bony. He had a couple of days of grey growth on his chin which certainly didn't match the dyed brown hair on his head.

Hugh Fraser.

"Can I help you?" he said, unsmiling.

Connor halted a metre or so away. "I'm Connor Reardon, and this is Gypsy Shields. I'm an investigator ex Homicide."

Fraser crossed his arms. "I wondered when one of you would show up. In it for the money? Not good enough for the cops anymore?"

Heat flushed through Connor's body. A muscle in his jaw twitched. "You knew we were coming. Was that before or after you buried the body?"

Fraser thrust his chest out. "If it's going to be like that, you can leave now."

"Did you know your friend's wife disappeared recently? Jarrod Whitehouse's wife?"

"Bloke up the road in security, Terry, heard from Lisa Riley, Lauren's other sister. Said she'd disappeared and they wanted an investigator. He asked around and your name came up."

"I don't think I've met him. Terry got a surname?" Connor said.

"You probably haven't but news travels. Word on your case close rate is it's high, unnaturally high, and maybe you have shall we say, an unfair advantage."

Connor wanted to punch the sneer off Fraser's face, but instead, he clenched his fingers. Obviously, this was how Elizabeth Metcalfe had originally found him. He rubbed at the back of his neck, stiffness intensifying. "Look, we're not here to make trouble. We hoped you might answer a couple of questions."

"Do you mind if we come inside?" said Connor.

Gypsy remained silent beside him.

Hugh Fraser put his hands on his hips. "Actually, I do mind. What's going on? As far as I'm concerned, Lauren's run off. They weren't exactly poster people for the perfect marriage."

"Jarrod told you about the marital problems?"

"Briefly. Did you find who she's having it off with yet?"

"Let's not get ahead of ourselves, and that's confidential information."

"Not when you're standing on my property it isn't."

"Mrs. Whitehouse was reported to police as a missing person a couple of days ago. So, either you talk to us, or you talk to the police."

"How did you tie me to Jarrod? The business deal? Remember I'm the victim here."

"How do you figure that?"

"Last year, I barely escaped with my life. Trespassers shot at me. Business deal gone wrong."

"Yes, we heard about that," Gypsy said.

Connor turned and gave her a warning look. He didn't want to alienate yet another witness

"I bet you did. The media story not the real story." Fraser had moved away slightly, glancing at his home at the bottom of the long driveway. "I only just made it."

"Through the underground tunnel," Gypsy said.

Connor cleared his throat. "I understand you were shot at, and some people were charged. I'm interested in how you knew Lauren Whitehouse."

"If you know about the business deals that went south because of a couple of criminal types, then you probably know I met Jarrod Whitehouse a couple of years ago, through friends."

"Which friends were they?"

"Is that relevant?"

"It might be. Lauren hasn't been seen for more than four days now. Her car is still in the driveway, and she hasn't used her credit cards."

"I see." Fraser's voice deepened. He continued to stare at Connor. "Lauren's a good woman."

Is or was?

"Regarding the payments Hugh Whitehouse made to you."

"That's private business."

"Maybe. Like I said, I can ask the questions, or cops can ask the questions."

Fraser stuffed his hands into his pockets, rocking slightly on his heels. "Yeah, but if the cops come calling, I'll ask my lawyer to the party."

"You need a lawyer?"

"Look, I'm not interested in your fishing expedition, okay? My private business is exactly that, private."

Connor considered the situation. He hadn't been asked to leave yet. He'd completed pissed off not only Jarrod Whitehouse but now Hugh Fraser. It was time to ease off the throttle.

"I'm sorry, you're right. I started off on the wrong foot here, and I've caused offence. As you can imagine, I'm anxious to find Lauren."

Fraser's shoulders relaxed, just slightly. "I thought they'd get divorced before she'd disappear. I know things were rocky with her and Jarrod but I thought they'd got over that. I don't get it."

"Have you heard from any of the creditors again?"

"Creditors?" Fraser snorted. "That's one word for them. That bastard builder is up on attempted murder charges. And no, I haven't heard from them again, thank God. "

"Did you consider moving?"

"I did, but then I figured why the hell should I run? Yes, there were problems with the development, but I did everything I could to work that out, to make it right with investors. That builder is a complete nut and deserves to be charged."

The conversation needed steering toward the area where Fraser might slip up. Judging by the colour in his face and his wide-open staring eyes, he was close.

"Was Whitehouse an investor in any of those properties?" Connor knew that wasn't the case but sometimes, a change of direction just might recover the situation.

"Nah, we were going into a new venture together."

"What type of new venture?"

The colour in Fraser's face had subsided a little.

"We talked about it. I recommended shares, but he wanted retail." Fraser stared off into the distance. "I told him there was no money in retail. I wondered if he was a frustrated retail fashion buyer, part of his alter ego"

Connor cast a sideways look at Gypsy.

"What do you mean by that?" Connor said.

"Maybe he means Jarrod looks good in clothes, pretty clothes," Gypsy said, her voice low.

"He likes his clothes." Fraser turned away from them. "I need to get back to what I was doing. You took me by surprise, turning up here without warning."

"You were referring to Jarrod's secret?   Is he

keeping up the blackmail payments? Because if not, you can tell us about it, can't you?"

"Get off my property, now," Fraser growled, turning back to point at Connor.

"What about the underground cellar. Maybe Lauren's hiding down there" Gypsy said with a sly smile

"You're a nut lady. Leave now and don't come back. This is none of your damn business." Fraser stormed down the driveway, toward his home.

"It is our business, and its Lauren and Jarrod Whitehouse's now. Is she in the tunnel, Hugh?" Gypsy called out to him, her neck straining.

Connor grabbed her by the elbow and steered her toward the top of the driveway, where their car waited just metres away

"Let's go. That's all we're going to get for now," he muttered.

A bang emanated from the front porch at the bottom of the driveway, but neither of them looked back. Connor unlocked the car with a click, and they swung themselves into the vehicle in a hurry. He pulled the seatbelt across and started it. He was rewarded by a roar from Black Betty. After turning the car around, he was rewarded with a squeal of tyres after he jammed his foot on the accelerator and took off at speed. They headed for the end of the street and got back onto the main road.

Neither of them spoke for a long time, until they were back on the freeway heading toward Brunswick. Connor by that stage felt his temperature return to normal.

"So, what now? "said Gypsy "You've got pretty much nothing out of either Fraser or Whitehouse."

"I know, but I didn't expect much more. If Fraser was blackmailing Whitehouse, neither of them will admit to it. "

"There's proof, though. You found it." Gypsy rubbed her index finger across the indent in her chin.

"I found proof that Whitehouse paid around ninety grand to Fraser, which according to the refinance on his mortgage, was supposed to be for renovations. I didn't see any renovations so I figure its hush money. I have the photos of Whitehouse in women's clothing, and plan on putting my theory to Ryan so he can take it further, but only once I get the client's okay. Then if charges need to be laid, Ryan can set it in motion. I wouldn't mind a look at that tunnel, though."

"Me, either. Can you prove the blackmail?"

"Well, not technically, although it might be fraud on Jarrod's part. Ryan can find out if it can be reported to the bank and take it from there."

Gypsy didn't reply. Connor flicked a glance at the sat nav to his left. They'd be home in around twenty minutes. He needed thinking time, and then to talk to Ryan and his client, Elizabeth Metcalfe. He had some information, but not what his client wanted, the whereabouts of her sister, alive or dead.

They drove on in silence.

"That tunnel's pretty curious, an unusual thing to have almost like he planned something" Gypsy said at length, turning her eyes. She had the look when she was hatching a plan, a sly smile.

"Whatever you're thinking, we can't do that, Gypsy."

"Why not? If Ryan questions him, there's no harm

in looking around the property."

"Other than trespassing."

"A minor inconvenience. If she's in there. can you tell yourself you didn't want to break the law to check?"

An incoming call rang through the car's interior phone. The small screen in front of him said 'Ryan mobile.' Keeping his hands on the steering wheel, Connor pushed a button in the centre of it and answered the call.

"Hello?" Ryan said.

"How's it going?" Connor said. "You're on speaker phone. Gypsy's in the car too."

"Okay, mate. Where are you? I know I asked you to come to my place, but I thought I'd drop by, better in person than phone." Ryan said.

In person visits usually meant he didn't want the conversation logged or traced officially on his mobile phone.

"Half an hour, maybe less," Connor said.

Gypsy watched him, scrutinising his face.

"Right. See you there about three then." Ryan hung up.

"Sounds juicy," Gypsy said.

"Maybe."

Connor tasted bitterness on his tongue, and at the back of his throat. For the first time in two years, the desire for a drink seared through him. Just one, to take the edge off, maybe a Bourbon and Coke, or a Jim Beam. Something sweet, dark, and potent.

He'd never been an alcoholic, but he'd drank in his younger days, to obliterate the memories and forget, a temporary anaesthetic. As he progressed through the police force into more senior roles, he'd turned to running rather than grog, to clear his head and purge the thoughts and pictures, a mental reboot.

But he hadn't gone on a run for over a year now. And rather than a long jog, what he wanted now was to feel the slow sweet warmth of the bourbon making its way down his windpipe, seeping through his chest into some burning reassurance.

"I might go out with Ryan for a bit when he gets there," he said

"Cutting me out of the action, huh?"

"I need to focus. Not cutting you out, hon."

But he was, and they both knew it.

He pushed another button on the steering wheel and the radio came to life, a classic rock station at low volume. Thankfully, Gypsy didn't press the point of him cutting her out of the investigation any further, and they arrived home before long.

He pulled up past Ryan's car already parked on the street and removed the keys from the ignition. As he opened the door, he caught a waft of warm summer air combined with a sprinkling of recent rain. He followed Gypsy up the steps to the front door and the slam of a car door a couple of houses down followed by purposeful boots striding their way told him Ryan hadn't come to ask after their welfare. He wanted information.

His son-in-law appeared at the bottom of the driveway as he pulled the screen door open.

"Hey, how's it going?" Connor said, facing him as Gypsy disappeared inside the house. "Yeah, okay, one of those days." Ryan's expression turned serious, mouth down turned and eyebrows gathered in.

"Come in," Connor said.

Ryan followed him into the hallway.

"We might head out for a bit," Connor said, projecting his voice into the living room where Gypsy flicked through some papers and leaned back on the couch. She turned her head.

"Whatever floats your boat," she said quietly.

"We'll only be an hour at the most." Connor turned toward the front door. "Let's go."

"We just got back!" said Gypsy, but wondered if maybe Ryan had something important to say, it wasn't like him to change plans this suddenly.

They left, stepping down toward the driveway where Ryan paused. "Your car or mine?"

"Mine. Let's go for a drive." Connor unlocked it.

They both got in, and he turned his head to reverse the vehicle. As they drove, Connor waited for Ryan to break the silence. As Ryan was the sworn in officer, Connor decided the direction of the conversation would be Ryan's call. The ever-increasing tendency to relive the plus points and minimise the minuses of his police career had remained flattened within Connor's chest for some time.

He swung the steering wheel, and the car bottomed into the steep driveway of Caraway Park, cricket nets and playing fields eight hundred metres to his left, tennis courts almost a kilometer down the driveway, and a large expanse of grass and trees to the right. He pulled into a parking space on his right, the only vehicle parked amongst ten empty spaces. He tasted the irony of a warm sunny day without a cloud on the sky, while he suspected bad news perched on the edge of Ryan's tongue.

He turned off the ignition. Silence settled in the car. Connor shuffled around in his seat, turning slightly toward Ryan who had curled inward, shoulders rounded and stare focused on the tumbleweed of hair on the car floor mat.

"So, what gives?" said Connor

Ryan lifted his chin and stared through the windscreen, across an expanse of lush grass to the bending saplings at its border. "A body turned up."

Connor waited.

"I wondered if it was this missing woman, you know, your crazy client's sister?" Ryan's lips twisted, before he rubbed at his mouth. He lifted his head to look at the rear vision mirror rather than the floor.

"How do you figure that? You never met her." Bile rose from his stomach, and a flicker of heat ignited in his gut. Intuition told him a body had been found.

"The night the loose cannon attacked you."

"What about it? You mean the night you and Gypsy closed ranks to try and shut me up in a hospital?"

"Shit, how's this weather where did it come from?" Ryan rubbed a palm across the right leg of creased black pants, and then tucked the hand under his armpit.

A pathetic attempt from Ryan at changing the subject and not answering the question. "Probably the same place you ID'd my client's sister, outta nowhere. Probably didn't have her purse on her, right?" He blew out a breath, his mouth forming an O, and then slammed the steering wheel with his open hand. Ryan must have been snooping through his case files to have the information he did. He hadn't told him.

"It's our job to join the dots, remember?" Ryan said quietly. "That's all this is."

"'Course it is. Every cop can't look his father-in-law in the eye, and the only reason is 'cause he's done his friggin' job. Don't insult my intelligence." Connor pinned Ryan with his gaze.

"This game's an exercise in frustration, I get it, but no way in hell am I letting you pin this one on me. Wrong target, Connor." Ryan scowled.

Connor put both hands on the steering wheel, pulling his shoulders back to stretch them. "Whatever. Why would you tell a PI that's sold their soul to the devil, otherwise known as clients, about the discovery of a body?"

"I give a shit, that's why. Closure for the family, locating a suspect within 24 to 48 hours of a crime scene." Ryan's face reddened, and the muscle in his right cheek pulsed. "She's in her forties, blonde. If I can get a copy of Lauren's photograph, and your client can identify her..."

"You probably already have it. You snuck a look in one of my files, right?" Connor shook his head. "I'll have to talk to Elizabeth. She'll most likely identify her"

"I could lose my job for telling you this."

Connor glared at him. "Where's the investigation at?"

"Forensics are all over it. Until they're done, we've got Buckley's chance of getting anywhere near it. I could get you maybe up to the tape, but you don't know about this, so..."

"How was she found?" The oil slick in his gut had spread, its dark edges slithering upwards.

"Guy walking the dog. Shallow grave, the dog sniffed out the tip of a finger poking above the earth. Out at Wilson's Point, half an hour past Rosebud."

"Time of death?"

"No idea yet, but a bit of info is filtering out. Word is she might have been there three days. Possible head injury. Cause of death looking like suffocation."

"Holy shit." Connor's throat ached. "Start talking to Jarrod Whitehouse. I did a some digging and found a series of payments to a builder over the last few months, Hugh Fraser."

"Okay." Ryan hung his head, his voice a low rumble.

Connor paused. "Not small change either, more than a hundred grand. Murder for hire, blackmail, or at best, fraud. A supposed refinance for renovations."

"Evidence?"

"I'll have to talk to my client first. Technically, the findings are hers, but I haven't had a chance to go over it with her. No time like the present, I guess."

Connor lifted the phone from the holder beside the steering wheel and swiped the screen. His habit of speaking to clients on speaker phone would be cast aside for now; letting Ryan listen in on phone conversations would be pushing the friendship past the boundaries of progressing the case.

Ignoring Ryan's round eyes and parted lips, he held up the index finger of his left hand as he dialed the number.

Elizabeth Metcalfe answered, her voice croaky. "Connor?"

"I have some information for you."

"You do?" The pitch of her voice swung upward at the end, her gasp breaking through the receiver.

"It'd be better in person, if possible. Can you drop

in to see me?"

"I'm picking Raleigh up after work today. His car's in for a service. I can drop in to see you after that, say around 4.30?"

Connor checked the time on his watch. An hour and a half away.

"Yes, I'll be there," he said. "I have a favour to ask."

She paused. "What kind of favour?"

"I have a contact in the police force. He's asking for a photograph of Lauren. I've also discovered some financial...irregularities. Giving him a copy of the information may progress the case, but I need your permission before I do that."

Her voice shattered, splintering and falling like rain on glass. "Oh, god. They've found her"

Connor paused before speaking quietly. "Nothing is confirmed. Best to take things one step at a time... I'll see you soon. "

"I'll kill that bastard I swear..."

The snuffling of her breathing combined with the cauterised pitch of her voice meant Connor had to hold the phone a couple of inches away from his ear.

"Let's not get ahead of ourselves," he said. "The case is progressing, step by step. Don't jump ahead on me, okay? Do I have your authority to pass this information on to my contact in the police force?"

"If the police don't include my bastard brother-in-law. He deserves to hang."

"No, not your brother-in-law, someone I trust, working in CID."

"All right."

Connor opened his mouth to say goodbye, but she'd hung up.

He sighed. "I need a drink"

Ryan lifted his head "Huh? Did you say a drink?"

"Yeah."

"Haven't seen you knock one back in a while." Ryan's eyes glittered.

If he wanted to know what was going on in his head, Ryan could join the queue.

"Today I need a drink," Connor said.

The next unsavoury task would be to ring Helen Reeves, wife of Joe Reeves, the bastard that smashed him in the back of the head. Whoever questioned Jarrod Whitehouse would be interested to see the photos of Mr. Reeves, with Jarrod in the background. Cross dressing plus large payments to Hugh Fraser for services unstated could prove motive at the very least.

Maybe Lauren discovered his secret and they argued about it. Whitehouse killed her during a tussle and buried her in a shallow grave. Either that, or Hugh Fraser found out about his penchant for dressing up in women's clothes and threatened to reveal Jarrod's secret. Why he would approach Hugh Fraser to kill his wife, he hadn't quite deduced, but Ryan and contacts would put him under enough pressure that they'd squeeze it out of one or both of them.

He turned the ignition and put the car into reverse.

"Where to?" Ryan said.

"Sportsman's Arms." He wanted to sit somewhere seedy, a rough hotel unfrequented by cops.

"Mate, you're driving."

"You can drive us home. I'm not planning on downing a dozen, more like one or two."

They left the park, and he turned right. They

would reach the freeway in a couple of minutes. Given the time of day, traffic would be light.

"What's up with this Fraser character?" Ryan said. His shoulders had dropped from beside his ears, and both hands rested on his thighs.

"Builder. Hit the media about a year ago, when he bailed and left investors in the lurch, payments but unfinished building. One of them rocked up at his place and shot at him. He escaped through an underground cellar."

Ryan shifted toward Connor. "An underground cellar, that's a new one."

"Isn't it? After I asked too many questions, including asking to see the cellar and tunnel he escaped through, he cracked the shits and told me to get off his property, saying it was all a private deal. Pretty much the same response I got from Whitehouse, but I didn't expect much else."

"Nah. Remind me of why we're on our way to one of the grungiest pubs in Melbourne at 3 o'clock in the afternoon?"

"A drink or two won't hurt. I've had my fill of crazies this week. The sharp edges need a bit of alcoholic sandpaper and there won't be many cops at the Sportsman's Arms."

Ryan rubbed his fingers across the stubble on his chin.

After a decade in the force, Connor wondered when the durable shell he'd accumulated had cracked. Sure, he'd been attacked by a man experimenting with his sexuality, had met with a frantic sister, investigated a frazzled cop nearing retirement and his shady business pal, and in an hour and a half, would ask Elizabeth Metcalfe to identify a body, probably the body of her murdered sister.

So why was he so angry and out of his comfort zone here? Could it be that his own conflict about what he could do and his own abilities as a Sentinel was getting to him?

It wasn't like he hadn't been in stressful situations before. The unpredictable nature of being a business owner didn't help. The insurance company, previously a steady stream of income, had asked for a brief hiatus of four weeks in their fraud investigation schedule, for reasons unspecified. They hadn't given a reason, and it gnawed at him. He wondered now if Hugh Fraser found out about his abilities maybe the insurance company as well, and he'd lost a pocketful of steady cash as a result.

He applied the brakes at the punt road freeway exit. Clients paid well for his services, but there was something to be said for a regular pay cheque from Victoria Police, even if the bureaucracy of said force jarred.

Ryan broke the silence. "Pondering a career change?" "It's crossed my mind once or twice." Being the driver had its advantages. He didn't want to look his son-in-law square in the eye.

"It has? First time you've admitted it."

Connor turned the heater on to a low setting. "I know Gypsy would rather I stay out of the force. We've both got used to me being at home at the same time, but I'm not sure how much longer I can stick in with this entrepreneur game. Something to be said for a cop's wage. It's not flash, but it doesn't change from week to week."

"They're looking to add to the team at CID."

"I know, you already said." The keys hanging from

the ignition jingled as the car accelerated. Black Betty's brute force comforted him, lulled him back into some sense of normalcy, if such a thing was possible.

"Don't leave it too long. They'll hire someone else."

Connor rubbed his fingers along the steering wheel. "I said I'll think about it. Talk to me once this case plays out, and I can see clear."

Thankfully, Ryan left it at that.

Connor flicked on the indicator to turn left into the pub car park. Only a few vehicles dotted the parking area. He pulled in and turned off the car.

"Can't wait to explain this to my team leader. Visiting the pub on a Thursday afternoon, all in the name of identifying a body."

Connor snorted as he climbed out. "The burdens of solving a case."

"You owe me one."

"I'd do the same for you."

"Let's hope it never comes to that," Ryan said. He strode beside Connor, his boots clipping the concrete.

When they stepped inside the pub, Connor squinted as his eyes adjusted to the dimly lit drinking cave. Hops and stale cigarette smoke hit him in the face.

"No shortage of seats. How about the booth in the corner?" Connor said.

He tried to ignore the stickiness of the carpet. The wooden table had seen better days, and the green vinyl bench seats was ripped in places. Definitely not one of the trendier pubs in town.

"What'll it be? Better be a good one to break the drought." Said Ryan

Connor suppressed a wry smile. The lure of a bourbon and coke had tugged at him for days. He couldn't let himself down by choosing anything else.

"Bourbon and coke please."

Ryan raised his eyebrow. "Bourbon and Coke, and a diet Coke it is." He placed both hands on the table and pushed himself up to exit the booth.

"Diet Coke? Wussing out on me?"

"Technically, I'm on duty, remember?"

Ryan walked off to the bar. Connor realised he'd put a dark raincoat on, possibly to cover up his uniform. The thought of reliving the memory of drinking alcohol didn't dent his conscience. He'd earned it. Considering most cops drank a hell of a lot more than one or two drinks, he wondered why Ryan made such a big deal out of it. Yeah, it was 3.30pm on a Thursday afternoon, but there were worse things he could be doing.

He should probably start up running again but motivation had deserted him long ago. Running was always associated with a day on the beat, to relieve the pressure of another day dealing with the dickheads at the top. Somehow, it didn't seem right to allow himself the luxury of a run when he'd shifted to the dark side, private investigation. It made no sense, but life generally didn't play strictly by the rules of logic.

Ryan approached the table with two drinks. He slid into the booth, took a sip, and looked at him with fingers interlaced.

"What, should I sell tickets?" said Connor, propping himself up moving one elbow to the table.

"Not paying a cent. I took a couple of hours off for this. Let's see what you got."

"There are worse things than having a drink, it's

not like I'm snorting a line off the table."

Ryan snorted. "Not sure I'd pay to see that, either."

Connor took a swig of his drink, savouring the feel of the warm liquid sliding down. Within seconds, it all come back to him, his muscles unknotting, and the blanket effect of thoughts switching off. A whole lot easier than running.

"What's the plan?" he said, leaning forward with both elbows on the table.

"I'll make a call. Whitehouse will hang up and call the union, probably on speed dial."

"Or you could use what I so generously gave you as leverage."

"Maybe. Or I get sprung for aiding and abetting a drunk."

"Ease up, I've got a way to go yet."

"You got fifteen minutes."

"Will you invite him for a pleasant chat down at the station?"

"That's the boss's call, not mine. Word is plenty would line up to see him in lockup for the night."

"Yeah." Connor drained his glass, and then placed it back on the table with a clunk. "Come on, you're not keeping up."

"I'm not on the hard stuff."

"Not sure that I'd call a bourbon with coke hard. More like a shot of tequila. Speaking of which..."

"We're outta here." Ryan shuffled along the seat and stood up. "This is getting ridiculous. The sooner we get back, the sooner we can put the hard word on Whitehouse."

Connor wondered why he'd ended up at a bar on a whim. He tried not to think about the spur of the moment events. He'd surprised himself. The force with which he'd fought back at Joe Reeves had overtaken him, almost from nowhere. The hidden reserve of anger had spewed forth; from a dark place, he didn't know existed. Maybe that was what propelled him to the bar for some reason, hidden away, a return to the days of old when drinking had been part of his promotion to detective.

Plus, he and Ryan very rarely disappeared on their own to speak without their spouses. He needed time to think, somewhere different, which might get ideas sparking.

"And the sooner I get to ring Helen Reeves. Gimme a minute, will you?"

He didn't have Helen Reeves on speed dial. Groaning as he pushed himself up and out of the booth, he headed for the main entrance to cut down on the noise of the bar. Striding toward the car, he pushed the automatic unlocking device and got in.

"Wait up, will you?" Ryan said, out of breath behind him.

Connor started up the car and scrolled through his phone to find previously placed calls. There it was. He pressed the screen, and the Bluetooth activated itself. Shit, Ryan would get to hear this one, but then he might be on the scene to witness the aftermath.

"Hello?" the woman who answered sounded tentative.

"Mrs. Reeves?"

"Yes, who is this?"

"It's Connor Reardon. I investigated that rather delicate matter on your behalf."

Her words came out in a rush. "Oh, my goodness, I'm so sorry. So, so sorry. I had no idea..."

"Me, either," he said. "How are you doing?"

He couldn't bring himself to ask about the wellbeing of his attacker.

"I'm okay. John's out of hospital, but he's angry and talking about pressing charges. We argued, and he took matters into his own hands. I wish I'd kept my mouth shut, but it turned out more difficult than I thought."

Perfect, just perfect. To top the day off, he could be served with papers for an assault charge if the peon went ahead with his plans. Then again, talk was cheap.

"I'm not calling about that. I'm calling about another case. One of the photos I presented to you showed a person in the background, a person who is likely a suspect. I'd like your permission to pass it on to police?"

"Police?   Oh, I'm not sure about passing confidential information on to police..." She loudly cleared her throat.

"I can assure you that the focus is not your husband. The focus is resolving a murder case. It is a matter of life and death. It is going to a specific contact, who I trust implicitly. You have my word on that."

"Well, I don't know..."

"You'd be helping a family bring closure to the disappearance of their sister and daughter."

A long pause.

"When you put it like that…" Helen Reeves' voice trailed off.

"Can I tell my contact you don't mind? That you'd be happy to be of service to the grieving family?"

"I guess." Her voice faltered.

"I'm sure they'll appreciate it, thank you."

Helen Reeves didn't reply. Now was not the time to remind her that if her husband laid charges, his lawyers would be sure to bring up all the sordid details of the investigation she had asked him to complete on her behalf.

"Okay, well, I guess you'll let me know if it helps. Bye for now."

His phone beeped as she ended the call.

"You know how to play the trump card, eh?" Ryan did little to hide his smirk as he steered the car onto the freeway.

"Whatever it takes, mate. Whatever it takes." Checking his watch, he calculated they'd be back in less than ten minutes, which would give him time to prepare for the arrival of Elizabeth Metcalfe, and possibly her husband.

"Will I come in, or wait out the front while you get the info to me?" Ryan asked.

"Just pull into the driveway. I'll bring it out to you after you switch cars. Elizabeth will probably want to meet me at the Coroners' first thing."

"I can meet her there."

"I know you can, but she's my client. She'll expect me to appear."

They drove in silence, Black Betty purred loudly, swaying as they followed the traffic to reach the back streets of Brunswick.

"Here we are." Ryan parked the car in the driveway, and rolled his shoulder around to face Connor. He twisted his wrist and tugged at the ignition, and lock and extended an arm out to Connor. "The keys to the vault."

Connor grabbed them and stepped out of the car.

"Won't be long."

He made his way to the front porch. He pulled open the screen door and turned the knob to open the front door, to be greeted by Gypsy, just inches away from where he stood.

"What was that all about? Since when do you do Bros before hoes? Both of her hands were firmly planted on her hips.

"Business," he said, moving to the left, meaning to climb down the stairs and into the bedroom.

"Oh, yeah? What type of business?" She tapped her foot on the tiles, in a slow rhythm. "You smell of bourbon"

"Is it a crime to have a drink? Last time I checked, it was still legal."

"I can't remember the last time you went out for a drink in broad daylight. What's going on?"

He pushed out a breath and shook his head. "I told you, business is going on. Don't get the wrong idea, please."

She folded her arms over her chest. "For God's sake, go and do something about your breath! Your clients will be thinking they employed a lush for an investigator."

"Exactly what I was planning to do already, but yeah, thanks," he muttered.

"I heard that, and no, the last thing I need is to babysit you. Get on with it!" She retreated into the house, presumably to reinstall herself on her laptop perched on the dining room table.

He quickly brushed his teeth, then dropped into his office chair and flicked open the folder for the Metcalfe investigation. He located the photos and the reports he'd printed out from the research software he'd gained use of as part of his contract with the insurance company, shoved it into a folder, and headed back out to the driveway.

Ryan waited in his idling car, elbow resting on the open driver's window.

"Here you go."

He looked up at Connor and raised his eyebrow "Thanks. I'll let you know."

He started up the car and left.

###

CHAPTER 8

Passing over the only evidence he had was an important part of the process, but Connor couldn't shake the sense that his mission to find Lauren Metcalfe slipped further away with each minute that ticked by. Like outstretched fingers over a cliff reaching out to a desperate victim, he occasionally came close to finding the answer and contacting the truth, bringing a surge of confidence, but otherwise he sensed that as a lone wolf outside the force, he had little chance of success in a borderline criminal matter. He didn't have the resources or manpower to rapidly solve the case. It had been more than three days since Lauren's disappearance, and as most cops and watchers of cop shows knew, the first twenty-four to forty-eight hours were crucial. He had nothing other than a maybe.

Connor trudged back inside, making for his PC to check emails. As he landed in his silver office chair with full body weight on the seat, the awareness of his isolation grew, the silence overpowering. He clicked on the mouse to activate the screen almost half-heartedly, knowing there'd be enquiries from people who wanted information and follow up, but very few of them would be life or death matters as they had been as a Homicide Detective. He should have accepted his new vocation by now, having worked mainly in insurance fraud for years.

He clicked on a couple of enquiries, one of them a referral quickly answered, then he pressed a button to play back messages.

One was a nervous sounding male leaving nothing but a telephone number, and the other was a telemarketer with broken English flogging off printer cartridges.

Elizabeth's car slowed down as it reached the driveway, probably with her other half. This would be interesting. What kind of man married someone like Elizabeth Metcalfe? Did opposites attract, or would they be two halves of a whole, in complete sync with one another as some couples were?

He pulled the case folder close to his chest, gripping its edges, knuckles turning white. He hadn't done a death notification in years. His gut tightened, and he concentrated on slowing down his breathing. He turned to his right, staring through the window to watch their body language as they left the car.

The familiar figure clicked her beige heels down the driveway. A man followed on her left, shorter than her, with dark brown hair combed neatly across his forehead and moustache twitching below a neat nose. He wore a brown suit and carried a briefcase. He had deep trenches in his forehead. He raised his chin to scrutinise the exterior of the building.

After a pause, Connor climbed the three steps to

open the front door.

"Please, come in," he said.

A grey pallor had spread over her face, mouth turned down. The man he assumed to be her husband avoided eye contact, gaze fixed firmly on the ground.

"Please, take a seat," Connor said quietly.

They stepped into the office and sat wordlessly, Elizabeth perched on the edge of her seat, barely moving. The man curled his hands inward on his lap, examining his neatly trimmed fingernails.

"I've forwarded the photograph and the details of the financial irregularities to my contact in the police force." Connor returned to his office chair. "They'll take it from there, and I'll update you as usual."

"It doesn't seem real, none of it," she whispered.

"It won't. Please bear in mind that the deceased person may not be your sister. This is merely a process of elimination, a formality. I don't need to tell you this can be a confronting process."

"I'd like to get it over with as soon as I can. The not knowing is agony."

"I understand. I'll talk to the Coroner's office. Maybe I can schedule something for first thing in the morning. I'll confirm with you. If it's going ahead, can you meet me there at 9.30 tomorrow morning?"

"Yes." She bowed her head.

Mr. Metcalfe cleared his throat. "Would you like me there?"

"No," she said, but he extended his hand to her.

She gripped his fingers. Connor wondered if he saw a look exchanged between them, but he had probably imagined it. They weren't lovebirds, but then they'd been married for a fair few years, and the slow erosion of daily living could do that to a marriage.

"Oh, I'm sorry, I didn't think, caught up in my own thoughts. This is my husband, Raleigh." She gave him a sideways look before shifting her eyes back to Connor.

Raleigh tried a smile. "Most people call me Leigh. Raleigh is somewhat stuffy and formal"

Not to mention pompous. He detected a slight English inflection to the man's tone, quite posh, almost royal.

Opposites must have attracted, because he couldn't imagine Leigh Metcalfe wooing anyone, and he didn't think Elizabeth chased him, it wasn't her style. Pillow talk would be a stretch, most likely a Shakespearean monologue. What the hell did she see in him? The guy must have had something going for him. Connor snapped back into the present, not wanting his mind to speculate on the specifics.

"Thank you, Leigh. I wish we'd met in better circumstances."

"I concur," Leigh said, rubbing the soles of his feet across the carpet.

"Elizabeth, a question. Do any members of your family work in financial services?"

"Err, I think so. Why are you asking that? Don't you believe me? It's obvious that snake hurt my sister. If you won't take it further, I will. He'll pay for this one way or the other."

Connor placed both palms up on the desk. "Unfortunately, there's no evidence of that at present, although there is evidence of potential fraud."

She didn't miss a beat. "Lock him up and throw away the key. Shame we don't have capital punishment in this country."

Her cheeks flushed crimson.

"Take each day as it comes. Are there any financial services professionals in the family, or close friends that you know of?"

"My sister Katrina is a financial advisor, and Leigh is an accountant."

Leigh raised his head. "Although I focus more on project management these days. New legislation has been introduced, and it is now against the law for an accountant to give financial advice."

Leigh hadn't been offensive, but the guy rubbed him up the wrong way. He didn't get along with pompous types, far too condescending for him.

"What about Katrina? They were close?" Connor said.

Leigh snorted, and Elizabeth raised her eyebrow, turning her neck slightly.

"Sometimes, depends on which way the winds blowing, but I'm not the best person to ask. Do you have sisters?" said Elizabeth.

"No." Connor paused. "Katrina can be somewhat unpredictable?"

"On and off like a light switch. Youngest child syndrome. She's always played on it."

"I see. Would she mind if I called or dropped in to see her?"

"Probably not. Flash your wedding ring in her direction, and she'll tell you all you need to know and a bit more." Her lips pursed.

Connor knew that every person grieved in different ways, and if Elizabeth Metcalfe was grieving without having identified the body, she seemed to be dealing with the beginnings of grief with cynicism.

He passed a notebook across the desk to her. "Would you mind jotting down her details?"

"No," she said, fiddling with a charm around her neck.

She dropped the charm, picked up the silver pen, and wrote the details down with scrawling curly handwriting. When she finished, she spun the pen between her fingers the pen and looked at him, her blue eyes clear now, the trace of clouds having disappeared.

"9:30 am." Said Elizabeth.

"Yes. I'll call the Coroners shortly. Here's the address."

"I'll find it. It's not getting there I'm worried about. It's getting home in whatever state I'm in. If I'm not myself tomorrow, Leigh, you know why."

"I will," he said, his spine straight, almost like a rope had pulled his head upwards.

Elizabeth stood up, hitching her handbag up over her shoulder. "I'm not sure whether to thank you, or not. You've done exactly what I hoped for—we've almost got the answer the family needs—but somehow, the nearer it gets, the more I want to run. It's not what I thought it would be."

She turned away toward the stairs.

"I understand. Unfortunately, feelings like that are reasonably common. It's a confronting time."

Hopefully, not too confronting. Women crying on his shoulders made him nervous, but in this case, there'd be no way around it. He couldn't keep calling on Gypsy every time a client threatened to collapse into floods of tears.

"It is," she said, her voice muffled. "See you tomorrow."

She paused before she opened the front door.

Leigh reached out with one hand to guide his wife, a surprisingly affectionate gesture. "If you need to get hold of me, I'll be at our place in Sorrento tomorrow. I don't usually go there much anymore, but I need some time away until this is sorted."

"I might come down and see you when I can. Text me the address." Said Connor

"Bye," she said quietly and left through the doorway which Leigh held open for her. The door clicked as it closed before them.

Connor sighed and walked through to the lounge room. He felt himself unravelling, the first stray strands pulling away from his tightly bound exterior. Gypsy remained focused on the screen in front of her.

He took the seat next to her. She looked up, and he moved his hand closer to hers.

"What's wrong?" She knew him, like no one else could.

For a moment, he contemplated laying it all out, the self-doubt, reconsidering reapplying for a place back in Homicide, his first big case after three years as an Insurance drone. Then he reconsidered, clamping his mouth shut before speaking.

"It's over, for now."

"What's over?"

"Possible death notification. They found a body matching Lauren's description. Buried in a shallow grave." He focussed on a spot on the table, zoning out in a mental oasis where no thoughts registered, before gazing back into her deep brown eyes.

"The fingertips?"

"Poking up above the earth, like you said."

"Holy crap." She moved her hands away from the keyboard. "What now?"

"I need a distraction. Something that doesn't involve death or disappearances. How about we ask Leah if she'll look after Mark for a few hours? Dinner, just you and me."

"I like your thinking." She a smile appeared on her pale face.

He reached across and kissed her. "Want to give her a call?"

"Yeah, gimme a sec." She fished around in her handbag for her phone and swiped the screen.

He needed a shower to wash the grimy layer on his skin. Possibly not bona fide grime sitting at a desk for most of the day, but hunting the sleaze that did this had gotten to him lately, and he couldn't shake the physical sensation of being slimed. He headed into the bathroom and turned on the shower. Steam poured out into the room. He undressed and gasped as the hot water hit his body.

He thought about a backup plan, alternate motives and previously unconsidered suspects. If Jarrod Whitehouse squirmed his way out of the net, he'd look in other hiding places for evidence. Right now, that was Katrina, Elizabeth's sister.

If a wife suspected her husband of dodgy financial dealings, who would she turn to? Someone with knowledge of finances, and the laws relating to them. Which meant Lauren would have most likely confided in either Leigh or Katrina. He couldn't image Leigh the stuffed shirt being anyone's confidante, but one lesson he'd learned early one was that people's choice in friends and those they turned to in times of stress could surprise him. In-laws that worked in the field were nothing if not convenient.

If in doubt, he fell back on the tried and true method: his notes. He would scrutinise them next, along with the time track of what he believed had occurred.

Drying himself off, he dressed in a hurry. Gypsy called out to him from the living area.

Her footsteps echoed through the office, and she reached the bedroom.

"You look nice. Guess what?" She beamed, eyes bright. "Leah said she'll pick Mark up from child care today. We can go out whenever we like. Freedom!"

She extended her arms and spun around, before hugging him. The night lay before them, filled with possibilities. A night to themselves.

He kissed her forehead. "Great. I better brush my hair to keep my lady happy, then we can go."

He didn't usually admit to enjoying a night out, usually preferring the quiet comforts of home, but tonight, he needed it.

She kissed him full on the lips. "I'd like to introduce myself. Remember me? I'm your fiancé."

He grabbed her hand, gently guiding her toward his desk where he picked up his wallet and keys. "Let's go, honey."

"What, now? I need to get changed."

He grabbed her around the waist. "You're gorgeous just the way you are."

Her sweet breath hung in the air between them.

"You'd like good in a hessian sack, honey. Spontaneity is where it's at. We're out of here."

She laughed, and they headed out to the car.

Inside the car, she pulled on her seatbelt as he turned the key in the ignition "Where are we off to then?"

"It's a surprise," he said.

He smiled so much his cheeks hurt. They needed to enjoy themselves more, take time out. He resolved then and there to schedule in more alone time with Gypsy.

"Oh, I love surprises," she said and moved her right hand across to his left thigh. "You're going to spill the beans tonight, right?"

"If you play your cards right, I might," he said.

"Cheeky," she said, and shuffled in her seat.

He planned on taking her to Grossi's, a high-end restaurant in the city. An unplanned night out should wash away the intensity that came with focussing on a disappearance, most likely a murder. He hadn't visited the restaurant before, but he knew Gypsy loved going out for dinner.

"What's with the secret meetings with Ryan then?"

"I don't want to spoil the moment."

"But you're going to anyway, right?"

He sighed. "I need time, I'm a bit surprised at Joe Reeves, I almost killed him."

"Yeah, me too" said Gypsy. "Give yourself a break, you've got a lot on your plate." "

"I don't know what's happening there." Connor shook his head. "I wish you'd give yourself more credit. and I'll admit I don't give you enough credit for the good you've done with your abilities. A dog sniffed it out, tip of a finger sticking out of the earth under a tree in Wilson's point, out past Sorrento."

"Oh, God," she breathed. "The poor family. How did Elizabeth take it?"

"I didn't need to tell her they'd found the body. I asked for permission to show Lauren's photo to Ryan for ID purposes. She guessed the worst."

"She must be going through hell. If anything happened to Leah, I'd be gutted." Gypsy pulled a notebook from her handbag, and began writing. "To do list. I need to distract myself with something practical" she said "It helps

"Okay" said Connor and he rubbed at his chin, keeping one hand on the wheel. "I'm meeting her at the Coroner's in the morning so she can view the body. No one likes notifying family. She's a lot saner than I had her pegged for. She acknowledged the news didn't quite bring the closure she'd hoped for, but then she's probably still in shock." Gypsy turned a page, nibbling on her bottom lip.

"I almost feel guilty sneaking away for a night out when they're going through something like that." Connor flicked on the indicator to turn right.

"You can't fix the world in one night." She grimaced as she crossed out two items on her list.

Gypsy had always wanted to save the world, help the underdog, even if it had almost cost her life. It had almost come between them, although he didn't feel quite so confident anymore in his previous insistences she dampen down her abilities. He wouldn't forget the grief at almost losing her, the raw bleeding wound that had only just healed over.

"I know, but it seems so unfair I get to keep my sister."

"You feel things more than everyone else, Gypsy. Sometimes it's okay to switch off and forget about the bad things in the world That's what tonight is for, so let's enjoy it."

"Deal," she said, and snaked her hand up his leg.

"Easy," he said, smile widening.

A surge of desire shuddered through him. Their love life had fallen further down the list since Mark's birth, but with a bit of luck, it might make a comeback tonight.

He pulled into the restaurant parking lot. "Here we are."

It took a moment before she saw the beautiful façade of Grossi's.

"You're taking me to Grossi's? A keeper, that's what you are." She reached across to plant a kiss on his cheek.

He parked the car, got out, and opened the door for her, his salute to chivalry for tonight. As she stood up, he saw the twinkle in her eye.

"You've got that naughty look." She laughed, the sound bright and happy.

"What you going to do about it?"

"That's for me to know and you to find out."

They entered the restaurant, and while he wasn't a frequent visitor to places like this, he admitted that he looked forward to bringing her, a haven of ambient lighting and luxurious surroundings among the grinding routine of investigation.

The waiter looked down at a large book, guiding his finger to their names written in pencil.

"Mr. Reardon and Ms. Shields, this way please," said the stocky waiter, as he bowed his head. His dark slicked back hair contrasted with his white jacket and shirt, immaculately pressed. He escorted them to their table, and they settled in.

"I think I'll lash out and have the duck," she said.

"Excellent choice, Mrs. Soon-to-be Shields," Connor said.

The waiter poured the wine before he smiled and

then disappeared, and Connor leaned forward on the table.

"There's been quite a few developments today."

"Agreed," said Gypsy, taking a sip of wine. "Come on then, details please, you know you want to."

"Elizabeth Metcalfe and Helen Reeves gave permission to pass on the photographs and financial reports to Ryan. He'll work with the team to put the hard word on Fraser and Whitehouse."

She grinned. "About time. I hope they put the wind up them."

"I'd put money on it. In the meantime, I'll talk to Katrina, the other sister. She's a financial advisor. I figure if Lauren knew about her husband's shady deals, she would have talked to her sister-in-law about it."

"Stands to reason. Unfortunately, it might have got her killed."

"Maybe. In the meantime, let's eat."

After enjoying a sumptuous entrée and meal, and spending time with Gypsy talking about matters non-domestic, relief coursed through him. He felt the mental reboot taking place, his mind emptying of its usual crowded thoughts. As the evening progressed, his mind turned toward getting Gypsy home, offering her his undivided attention, and taking off her work clothes.

A muffled beep seeped out from her handbag.

"Sorry, I better check that," she said, resting her fork on her plate. "It might be Leah."

She brought the phone to the table and glanced at the screen. A text from her sister.

"Yes!" she said loudly. Heads turned, and she lowered her voice. "Leah's got the day off and she said we should enjoy the night out. Mark can sleep, over and I'll pick him up in the morning."

Connor grinned. "Excellent. In that case, we should leave as soon as possible so I can rush you home and demonstrate my appreciation for a night out."

They hurried through the rest of their meal eager for some time alone.

Finishing the chicken with brie, she wiped her mouth, and then dropped the napkin onto the table and pushed back her chair. "You don't have to tell me twice. Let's go home so I can remind you of the way things used to be."

Connor paid the bill, and escorted her out. After opening the car door for her, he drove home, trying not to break the speed limit.

Just inside the living room door, he dropped his keys and wallet onto the table and took Gypsy in his arms. Her soft lips and the delicate suppleness of her skin reminded him of all he had missed. He scooped her up and carried her to the bedroom.

"Let's make it a night to remember," he said, his voice gruff.

"If you insist." She smiled, the light glowing in her eyes.

He stopped as he reached the bed. A blonde-haired woman with a strong resemblance to Lauren Whitehouse waited for them. Lauren was nothing if not determined to get a message to both of them. She stood wearing what appeared to be work clothes: black skirt, dark jacket, and light blue shirt. She stood next to the bed as clear as if she had dropped in for a chat, but didn't appear to be speaking.

He released his tie and sat on the edge of the bed,

and rather than lying back to gesture for him to join her, Gypsy sat on the edge, feet flat on the floor.

"My god," she whispered. "Do you see that?"

Strangely, as their abilities were slightly different, they rarely experienced visions at the same time. "Yes," he said, barely moving.

What did she have to tell them? Could she solve the case, by revealing her killer?

She stood before them and for a moment, he wondered if she was real. She barely moved. Then she swayed a little, and smiled up at him, her eyes radiating kindness and goodwill.

"She likes you," Gypsy said. "If you weren't confident you were a Sentinel or a spiritual guard before now, I think this confirms it. I don't think she'll take no for an answer."

He couldn't look at her, fascinated by the figure barely a foot in front of him. He'd cringed if anyone had hinted the faintest idea of the supernatural while in the force, but then it wasn't exactly the environment for telling colleagues you saw dead people, sometimes the living in another location, and could break a psychic connection without too much effort.

Now word had got out that his Sentinel abilities played a big part in his case close rate, he had nothing left to hide. How many people knew he could cut communication between psychic mediums, and receive visions from both the living and dead? If he went back into the force, it would be with rumours swirling. The constant focus on his reputation drained him and at this present moment, he exhaustion crept through him.

"I'd love to investigate that tunnel of Hugh

Frasers. Did he keep you there, Lauren? Were you kidnapped?" said Gypsy.

Connor looked at Gypsy, chin out, leaning forward, desperate for answers. Lauren continued to smile and shook her head. No.

"Well, I'll be damned," she muttered. "So, who did this?"

Lauren took a step forward, lowering her ethereal form to the bed, slowly and gently. She turned to Connor and smiled at him. A rush ran through him, and he wondered if she could see into him, see every picture, every thought, every doubt. Maybe she'd see him as a fraud, inept and incompetent.

She stared at him and reached under her arm. What looked to be a blanket appeared at first, followed by a small bundle. Her head dipped, and she extended both arms out to him, gesturing down for him to look directly at what she held in her arms.

A baby. He froze. Was Lauren Whitehouse pregnant at the time of her death? If so, this changed everything, in particular Jarrod's claim she had been having an affair. Could there be something to his accusation?

"She trusts you," Gypsy said. "If a woman asks you to hold her baby, you know you're okay."

Awash with emotion, he moved his hands out to hers, and after a moment's hesitation, he lowered his hands to below her forearms, ready to take the baby she had offered.

She vanished, taking the baby with her.

Neither he nor Gypsy spoke, overcome with what had just occurred.

"That was intense," Gypsy said at last.

He still couldn't speak. With that one gesture, she

had told him all he needed to know. He should stop doubting himself, he wasn't the bumbling fool he thought he was. If he'd let this woman in, and received the vision earlier, rather than dismissing it as coincidence, the communication Lauren sent him might have saved her life. He might have saved her life.

"You're a good man, Charlie Brown," Gypsy said. "I know it, and so does Lauren Whitehouse. Trust yourself like she trusts you. Like I do. No more doubting your abilities."

The shackles of doubt fell away from him. He could help like no one else could, one of the only Sentinels he knew of in existence. It was time to make things right.

"Come here," Gypsy said.

She took him in her arms, and he allowed her to hold him, his head on her lap. He remembered everything he loved about her and why he'd been attracted to her at their first meeting. Despite his flaws and faults, she truly loved him.

Now that the biggest hurdle, his not trusting Gypsy with her abilities, had been smashed out of existence, he felt closer to Gypsy than ever before. There had never been anyone other than her, and never would be anyone else. Of that much he was certain.

\#

CHAPTER 9

If Connor thought the day before had been harrowing, he knew today, depending on the body identification, would be worse. His client collapsing into grief at the death of her sister could take his comfort zone and shift his confidence in his abilities as an investigator to an all-time high if he handled it right.

He'd steeled himself for the day ahead with the biggest strongest cup of coffee he could get his hands on.

At the Coroner's office in central Melbourne, he flashed his license at the receptionist sitting at the front desk and began to sign in.

"Morning, Connor," she said.

He looked up from the sign in sheet. "Cilla. You remembered."

"How could I not?" She flashed him a pearly smile.

Did she just bat her eyelashes at him? If she did, he wouldn't argue. A hidden benefit of going through the scene with the ghost of Lauren Whitehouse last night was not only a renewed strength in his relationship, but increased confidence, walking a little faster and a little taller.

"Judging by the look on your face, I'd say your headed up to the seventh floor."

"That obvious, huh?"

"I like a man who shows what he's thinking."

So much for his 'I'm a closed book' theory.

"Err, okay, Cilla," he said. "See you later, maybe."

He followed a balding man carrying a briefcase toward the six lift entry points, and pushed the button, shoving his hands in his pockets. He had searched for but not found Elizabeth in the foyer so maybe she was up at the seventh floor already. He squeezed into the lift and noticed he was the only one that got out at the coroner's floor.

He exited onto dark brown durable carpet. The narrow corridor continued for about fifty metres before he reached a sign saying, 'Identification Suite.'

It had been a long time.

He pushed open the glass door. Suzie the departmental assistant stared at the keyboard, tapping at the keys furiously. Connor stopped by the desk, and shifted his weight from his left to his right foot. She lifted her chin and smiled, exposing the new set of teeth she'd been spending her wages on back when he last saw her.

"Connor, how long's it been?"

"Nearly two years."

"Time flies." Her lips pressed together firmly. "You're meeting a family?"

"Unfortunately, yes. My client is Elizabeth Metcalfe. A body found at Wilson's Point."

"Okay. I'll go talk to a techie." She stood from her

chair. "Back in a sec."

She left, and a technician Connor recognised entered the small foyer area, Ethan Jenkins. Connor wondered if he was still popular with the ladies as he had been back in the day. He'd ribbed him repeatedly about the burden of women falling at his feet.

"Heard you were coming in." Ethan smiled and extended his hand. "Gone to the dark side, private investigation, huh?"

"Something like that." Connor shook his hand.

"Let's go. I'll run you through on the status before your client gets here, if you like."

"And if Elizabeth arrives?"

"Suzie will ask her to take a seat until you can get to reception to talk to her. I'm sure you know the drill. Maybe have a look first?"

"Yeah." Ethan took a couple of steps away from the desk and gestured toward the door to the right of Suzie's desk.

Connor's heels clacked across the light grey tiles of one of the coroners viewing rooms.

A sheet had been placed across the body on a table in the centre of the sterile and barren room, and as they walked through the door, the familiar smell of decomposition greeted him, a mixture of sewage, disinfectant, and decay. He'd never forget it., though, he had certainly tried to wash the smell off many times, unsuccessfully.

His shoes echoed on the tiles as he stepped toward the head.

Ethan pulled back the covering. Although he'd been certain the being that had visited him was Lauren Whitehouse, seeing her dead body struck him like a physical blow. Based on the photograph, the body before him matched the Lauren Whitehouse that had visited him in spirit form. Her face was beautiful in death, and she was unmarked. He tried to imagine her unconscious and buried in a shallow grave, a sleep that continued until her heart stopped beating and a shudder rippled through him.

"Can I see her fingers?"

"Yeah, although a lot of the fibres have been removed."

Ethan lifted her hand, and he imagined the loose earth covering her, covering her. At least she hadn't realised she'd been buried alive. Until the spirit left the body that is and she latched onto Connor, trying to get a message through to him, which at this point remained uncertain. They turned at a sound at the door.

Suzi's brunette head appeared around the frame of the door. "She's here."

Ethan and Connor exchanged a glance.

"I might come out and speak to her if you think that would help," Ethan said.

"If you could," Connor replied, glancing back at Lauren's face. "She was dreading it yesterday."

Ethan lifted the sheet back over the body and left, and Connor followed. They reached the family waiting area where Elizabeth sat hunched over, her pale grey suit matching the lack of colour in her face.

She looked up as Connor entered, and stood, stumbling. He placed his arm under her elbow. If he just focussed on each moment, the here and now, they'd both get through this.

"I'm not sure if I can do this now. I didn't sleep last night." Elizabeth covered her face with her hands.

"There's no rush. Take your time. Better to take

the time you need to prepare yourself now if you can."

She sniffed. "Thank you. I think I might go in and get this over and done with, at least that way we know one way or the other."

"Are you sure?" Connor said, scrutinising her face.

She nodded. "As ready as possible to view what might be my sister." She dropped her hands to her sides.

She walked toward the door, Ethan on one side and Connor on the other. They reached the large glass window, and she stared through it at the covered figure on the table.

"Take a deep breath," Ethan said.

She slowly parted her hands and peeked through her fingers. She lifted her head. and took a deep breath. "So far, it looks just like a sheet. If it is her, I can't think about what she went through"

Now was not the time to mention that she'd been alive when she was buried.

"We won't go in there until you give us an indication." Ethan said.

"Right." She took a long slow breath then tugged at her suit jacket. "I don't think there's ever going to be a right time to do this. Let's go in."

"We don't have to do this today. It's okay if you change your mind," Connor said. "We can sit back down and rethink this if you need to."

"It's not going to change anything." Her eyes didn't shift to Connor but remained focused on the large window. "I'm here."

Ethan moved first, pausing as he pushed open the door to the sterile morgue, watching her carefully.

"I'll go in first," he said. "You can when the time is

right."

She took her first tentative step, looking down at her shoes before shuffling along the window and reaching the door. She stepped through it and onto the tiles, her footsteps echoing through the cavernous room.

Connor thought about the time he'd last been in a tiled, soulless environment, when Gypsy had been in Intensive Care fighting for her life. Faced with the immediacy of the situation, the perspective of life had hit him.

"It all just got a bit too real," she said.

Connor remained beside her, wondering if he'd be the one to catch her if she fainted.

Ethan stood at the head of the body, one hand paused on the corner of the sheet. "You understand that if this is your sister, she will look different to how you remember her?"

"Yes, I understand. Is she bloodied and bruised?"

"No, she isn't." Ethan frowned, his mouth set in a grim line. His hand seemed frozen in place, not venturing to lift the sheet.

Elizabeth took a step closer to the table, staring at the body. Her attention moved to Ethan's hand.

"Lift the sheet, please."

He removed the sheet, and Connor focussed every ounce of his attention on Elizabeth Metcalfe.

"Oh, my God." Her voice cracked, and her knees buckled.

Connor bent slightly, catching her under her armpit before she dropped to the white tiles.

"That's her, my darling sister. What did he do to you?" She shuddered and crumpled, her knees moving closer to the floor.

Connor stretched out his other arm, reached for a chair, and scraped it across to rest behind her. He guided her into it and she sat, landing heavily He placed one arm on her shoulder.

"I'll drive her home. Can you arrange something with security as far as her car is concerned, please?" Connor said to Ethan.

"Sure." Ethan pulled the cover back over Lauren's face.

"I didn't drive," she squeaked. "I was going to catch the train to Sorrento. I don't know what I was thinking."

Her sobs increased in volume.

Connor waited as grief racked her body and her shoulders heaved. It took a couple of minutes before these quieted from obvious gasps to the occasional sniff.

When she paused to wipe her nose, he said, "How about I drive you back to Sorrento?"

"Yes, please. I'm going back to the holiday house."

"I'm sure we'll manage." He felt what probably appeared to be a pathetic smile cross his face.

Elizabeth may have noticed if she looked his way which she didn't, of course, too wrapped up in the cocoon of the far too real evidence of her sister's death.

She slowly raised herself from the seat, legs still wobbly. He extended his arm to catch her just in case she fell.

"I'm okay," she said. "I won't collapse on you."

It would certainly be a quiet drive, punctuated most likely by sobs and sniffs.

He placed his arm on her forearm and guided her

back out through the doors, walked through the corridor, and pushed the button on the elevator.

"We don't need to talk," he said, "just relax in the car as much as you can."

"Thank you. You've gone above and beyond the call of a private investigator, and for that I'm grateful."

"It's okay. Times like these are part of being human, and given the current situation, completely understandable."

Guilt moved through him, guilt at the gratitude he'd felt earlier at still having Gypsy with him. Elizabeth Metcalfe had just lost her sister forever, and if he had anything to do with it, she'd gain the closure she needed, identifying the person responsible for her death. A family had lost a sister and a daughter, and she would miss out on all those moments most people took for granted having a mother to guide and support them through.

They reached the car park, and once he settled her into the passenger seat of his car comfortably, he prepared for the drive of an hour and a half to Sorrento. Elizabeth didn't speak for the entire drive, lost in her own world of grief, and he wasn't about to begin a stream of inane chatter purely for the sake of something to say.

Eventually, they pulled in front of a quaint cottage, yellow with green shutters on the windows, and wild garden complete with rose bushes and wisterias. A silver Celica parked in the driveway with personalized number plates, NUMBER5. Normally, he'd view the location as a picture of serenity and relaxation, but the chances of his client gaining that today were close to zero.

She let herself out of the car and walked toward the front door. Connor followed behind her. He wanted to make sure she was okay, and get a look at the holiday home. The seed of an idea had formed in his mind but hadn't yet begun to sprout, intuition guided him. It hadn't let him down before and he wasn't about to do so now, even if it meant taking Elizabeth on a long drive. She turned the handle. "It's not locked. Leigh's home."

The hallway was short and led directly into a comfortable living area decked out with retro furniture and tasteful throw rugs and cushions.

"Sit down, I'll make you a cup of tea," Connor said, and he began the hunt for supplies in the small kitchen, recently renovated, by the look of it. After the tea was ready, he moved back to the couch, moving slowly to make sure it didn't spill.

He sat down beside her on the faded brown couch from the seventies. Her hair had escaped from her usual tightly restrained bun. She took off her jacket and kicked off her shoes. "Today was hell," she said quietly.

He wasn't sure how to respond so remained silent. After a moment, he said "Thank you for identifying Lauren. I know it wasn't easy, but now forensics can do their job. I'll work with them to find the person that did this."

"I did it for her, no one else. It's what she would have wanted. I don't know how I'm going to tell my parents, or Leigh, for that matter." Her eyes began to water again.

"Don't think about that now," he said, patting her arm. "Try and focus on making yourself comfortable. I'm sure you'll never be the same again, but it's probably best to focus on each day as it comes."

"Have you lost anyone close to you?" she said through tears.

"Yes, my brother, Dan, it's been years now. I'll never forget the day I got the news. The Russell Street bombing you probably heard it in the media"

"I did," she said quietly.

"Losing someone you love is devastating, and there's always a part of you that remembers. Of course, the memories never leave which is some consolation, but somehow, focusing on getting through each day helps."

"You understand." Her voice trailed off and she stared into the empty room.

"I deliberately didn't say I understand because so many people at the time told me they did. The truth is, I don't think anyone can truly understand what we go through. The best we can hope for is acceptance, and remembering all they brought into our lives."

He'd never tell her that the moment he'd lost his brother would be etched forever in his memory, the aching need never quite leaving. That the ragged, gaping open raw wound never completely healed, that it covered over slowly inch by agonising inch, and that although it had been more than fifteen years since he lost him, he thought about his brother nearly every day. The loss never went away, it simply faded with the passage of time.

"That's true," she said. "I hope I don't seem rude, but I think I might take your advice. I'm probably going to lie down."

"Good idea. I might go and talk to your husband before I leave."

Although Elizabeth had specifically asked Leigh to

stay behind, Connor had assumed that although a conservative type, he'd be waiting at the door for them, to ask how everything went. Even if he and Lauren hadn't got along, as was often the case with in-laws, wouldn't he want to know what happened? If nothing else, his wife needed his support now more than ever. He remembered the look between husband and wife in his office the day before. The marriage had probably decayed to a point of no return, crumbling into a state barely salvageable.

"He'll be in the den," Elizabeth said.

"Where's that?"

"Back of the house, down the corridor and to your right." She pushed herself up from the couch and padded away on stockinged feet.

He walked through the corridor. The second door on the right had been pushed ajar. Through the doorway, he saw Raleigh sitting in an office jar, a strong light and magnifying glass on a large desk of dark wood.

Connor tapped on the door. "Sorry to interrupt. I thought I'd pop in to let you know Elizabeth's home." Boxes were piled precariously on the old desk, some of them open and lined with ribbon and various adornments with coins and stamps nestled safely within them.

Leigh immediately stood, as if surprised. "Oh, I'm sorry. I hope you don't think me rude, I didn't hear the car pull up. This all proves a welcome distraction, as I'm sure you understand. It's a time of major upheaval, and well, when the going gets tough, the tough turn to their stamp and coin collection." Raleigh managed a thin smile.

"You're a collector?"

"Yes, I find it relaxing after dealing with the current stresses. Focussing on each piece's history and uniqueness seems to help me unwind."

"Looks like you've been at it for a while."

"I'm a part of the local club, and some of the pieces I've acquired are quite rare. Like this one for example. It's called a Penny Black. There's only a few left in existence."

He gazed down at a case which contained a black stamp, with a white silhouette of the Queen of England prominently featured.

"Worth much?" Connor said, leaning against the doorway.

"Priceless and absolutely rare. I'd never part with it, never."

"I see." Connor wondered where the hell an Accountant had got hold of priceless stamps, and had them squirrelled away to be admired at will. "Well, I'll leave Elizabeth in your care now. She seems to have recovered from the shock."

"I'll check on her now. It's been a very trying time for the entire family. Was the victim Laura?"

"Unfortunately, yes. A terrible shock."

Leigh's face paled. "Terrible news. Such a loss. She was such a bright outgoing person. Poor Elizabeth. I'll see what can be done for her."

Connor nodded and left the den. Elizabeth was nowhere to be found, so he let himself out. On the drive home, he thought about his life, the loved ones surrounding him—Gypsy, Mark, his daughter Christie, his son-in-law Ryan— and the luxury of spending time with them working from home. Some people lost those most precious, their loved ones. Each time he'd notified a family of a tragic incident, it had reminded him of how much he took for granted. His chest ached.

The beauty of Sorrento and the surf coast couldn't be ignored, even while driving. Waves surged against the rocks, and the sun peeked through clouds, creating a magical view. He took an occasional peek, once the curves in the road subsided.

He looked forward to seeing Gypsy and Mark, loosening up his tie and sitting back to spend the rest of the afternoon with them. He pressed the play button on the in-car stereo system and the soothing sounds of Santana filled the car, as he pulled up to the lights to enter the Geelong freeway.

While he was at the lights, he decided he'd give Katrina, the sister, a call from the Bluetooth within Black Betty.

She answered it on the third ring. "Wealth building systems, Katrina speaking."

"Katrina, it's Connor Reardon."

"Liz said you might call. You have a nice voice. Deep and rumbling."

"Did Liz mention the reason for my call?" he focused on the road ahead.

"Let's just say my sister and I aren't exactly close."

"I see. Did your sister-in-law ever express concern to you?" Connor tried not to react as an idiot in a red hatch back cut him off.

"About what?"

"Her husband's financial dealings, namely his payments to Paradise Investments a couple of months before her death."

"Yeah, I heard about that. She was a breath of fresh air. I take it you've met Raleigh? Let me tell you, we all dread being stuck next to him at a family function. Good for those of us that suffer insomnia, though." He turned his head to look for traffic in his lane as he entered the ramp to the freeway. He hit the accelerator and the Betty rumbled in response.

"Were you close to Lauren?"

"Kind of, although she was definitely a closed book. Weird talking about her in the past tense like that. It still hasn't sunk in, but then they say the grieving process takes time. Still seems like it's happening to someone else."

"Understandable."

"She did mention something unusual, though. She said she couldn't live with a man who preferred dressing up and experimenting to her."

"I see. Anything else occur that seemed unusual to you?" he sighed as he braked, flashing signs indicating roadworks ahead.

"Yeah, she said over her dead body would he get the house, and she mentioned a second mortgage or refinance that she wasn't happy about. Every time she asked when the renovations were going to happen, he made excuses. Some builder guy came over to see them but it was all talk."

"All right. Did you meet this builder guy?" Sunlight streamed through the windscreen and he rubbed his right hand down the last pair of faded jeans he owned.

"Nah, she said he was a bit older, though. I think his name was Harold or Hugh or something like that."

"Hugh Fraser?"

"Yeah, that's him. She said she was worried that Jarrod had siphoned off the money they refinanced and gave it to this Hugh character. Sounded dodgy as hell to me"

"Did you make any recommendations to her?" he gripped the steering wheel tighter.

"I told her if Jarrod was paying this Hugh character, and no building took place, depending on what was dug up, she could possibly have him done for fraud."

"Did she go any further with her enquiries?"

"I don't know. She disappeared not long after that. Last time I saw her, she was quieter than usual, withdrawn almost which wasn't like her. She'd had her hair done but she looked pale, pinched almost. I wondered if she was sick. Didn't ask her, though, thought it might worry her more, but she looked terrible."

"Did Lauren speak to your brother about her concerns?" He flicked on the indicator to change lanes.

"Hardly. In case you haven't noticed, he's not exactly Mr. Personality. He's a pompous old stuffed shirt. I don't know what Elizabeth sees in him. I can't imagine he'd be a tiger in the bedroom."

"They weren't close?"

"No. I'd like to get close to you though if that sexy deep voice is anything to go by."

Now he understood the oblique references Elizabeth had made earlier. Cougars weren't exactly on his wish list, and a woman like Katrina would be accustomed to getting what she wanted. Not in this case, though. He considered himself well and truly taken.

"Thanks for the information," he said, ignoring her advances. "It will assist with my enquiries."

"Okay, bye then. Maybe you could drop by in

person sometime soon, really soon."

Sheesh. The woman didn't let up. He gave her some begrudging credit; she was nothing if not persistent.

He hung up. The interview had rocketed from professional to ridiculous in a matter of minutes.

He looked at his watch. Still early afternoon.

Unlocking the front door and hanging up his car keys, he kicked off his shoes and lay back on the couch, allowing his thoughts to wander. Today's information provided conflicting lines of enquiry. Lauren knew about the blackmail and therefore her husband's secret, potentially opening her to foul play, but her pregnancy indicated an affair with person's unknown. Motives were aplenty, but evidence remained scarce.

Soon he'd go back to the timeline of events, and see what floated to the top as far as suspects went.

Given the lack of evidence tying either Whitehouse or Fraser to the murder, he needed to approach things from a new angle.

The room faded to grey. Next thing he opened his eyes to was a darkened room. Gypsy must have laid the blanket over him.

He pushed himself up from the couch. "Gypsy? You there?"

Her voice echoed from the kitchen, "Yeah, I'm here."

She walked over and stood beside him, an amused smile playing across her face.

He sat up on the couch.

"Bit of a nanna nap then?"

"I can't believe I fell asleep," he said, rubbing his face with his hands.

Shit, he should have been working on the case, not dozing off. He pushed himself up from the couch, throwing the blanket aside, and stood up. He massaged his lower back.

"Maybe you should take tonight off, take it easy for a change."

"Not sure about that. There's something I haven't found yet. I'm close. I can feel it. I tell you what, though, something smells good."

"I'm cooking dinner, your favourite, pasta carbonara."

"Great. I'll open a bottle of wine." He turned on the stereo and put on an L J Hooker CD.

The smooth tones washed over him and the muscles in his shoulders relaxed. He loosened his tie.

"I think I'll get changed," he called out to Gypsy who had got up and headed back into the kitchen. Once he put on his old comfortable clothes, the relaxation process began in earnest and the tension of the day gradually rolled away.

As he returned to the dining area, he reached the table and took a seat to the left of his son. Mark sat at the table in his high chair. Gypsy brought over a large steaming bowl and then sat down across from Connor. After the day that was, sitting with his family like this seemed like a welcome release, a return to the every day.

"Thanks, honey, this looks fantastic," he said, serving pasta onto his plate.

She placed a bowl of cooled pasta onto Mark's highchair and began eating.

After a few mouthfuls, she dropped her fork and said, "So, what's the plan from here?"

"I'll talk to Ryan. He'll be pushing through the

autopsy results as fast as he can. They've been fast tracked. Whitehouse and Fraser will be questioned."

"Oh, to be a fly on the wall," she said, her fork almost touching the bowl of steaming pasta.

"Ryan should call either after dinner or in the morning. He knows I'm waiting for the results. One plus side to today was the potential to gain fibres and other evidence from the body."

"Will Whitehouse be charged?"

"Hopeful, but still unknown. It all points toward fraud, blackmail maybe, but not murder. Ryan's best hope is for a confession, and I don't think it'll come easy." He grabbed a bread roll from the middle of the table and began buttering it.

"No." She tilted her head and smiled at him. "It's nice to have you with us, instead of locked up in your office."

"Yeah, part of my new plan."

"New plan?" she put a forkful of pasta into her mouth.

"To spend more time with my family."

"I like the sound of that." She smiled without baring her teeth.

"Thought you might." He smiled and wondered why they hadn't married.

It wasn't because he hadn't asked her. After she got out of rehab fully healed from the after effects of the shooting, he'd got down on bended knee to propose, and with tears of joy she'd said yes. Months later, when they'd set up a home together and after Mark's birth, he'd tried setting a wedding date. She'd brushed him off, claiming they didn't have the money for a wedding.

He knew it was more than that, and he didn't think

it was him, more like the idea of marriage. Being conservative, tied down, a middle-class existence didn't appeal to her the way it did to him. He wanted to hide and enjoy the comforts of home, but she still hung on to the streak of rebellion that ran in her a mile wide, especially the night they met. He should have known early on, when she'd put herself in harm's way during an attempted abduction in a bid to rescue the woman, that adventure and danger would follow wherever she went. Yet at some point, she'd need to reconcile the life they lived, with the future she didn't want to think about.

Tonight, with the music playing and the lights low, he watched her as she tenderly fed their son in between eating herself. Her brown hair fell across her forehead in waves, and her smooth skin begged to be touched. He reached across with and caressed her left cheek with his fingers. She turned her head away from feeding Mark and faced him.

"You really are beautiful."

She smiled. "What do you need help with tonight then?"

She had deflected yet another compliment, but he was onto her game. Warmth surged in his chest. He knew from the shine in her eyes and the slow smile spreading across her face that he just might win her over.

"Nothing, other than you."

"You need help with me? What?"

"All I want is you, Gypsy."

"You stole that from the song, honey."

"Marry me."

She moved closer to him, her face just inches from his. "I already said yes, remember?"

Then her soft delicious lips were on his. He luxuriated in their kiss, before Mark started yelling for attention. After a few more seconds, she pulled away.

"I better feed him then put him to bed," she murmured.

"Good idea," he said. "Let's talk when he's tucked in. The sooner, the better"

He stood up, scraping back his chair, and walked toward the office. He could look over the timeline of events while Gypsy settled Mark for the night.

Sitting down in his desk chair, he took the file and opened it. If the killer wasn't Whitehouse or Fraser, the someone else lurked within these pages.

He thought about Jarrod Whitehouse claims of an affair. If Lauren Whitehouse had an affair, could her lover be the killer? But why?

He had to face the fact that the dreams may have been a message from Lauren Whitehouse herself. If she was pregnant before she died, who was the father and why did he kill her? Maybe he wanted a termination and she didn't or vice versa?

Would that be a motivation for murder? Something else?

He grabbed his pen and wrote a list of possible motivations:

- Pregnancy
- Jealousy
- Wouldn't leave husband
- Money? What angle?

Who and where was this faceless lover? From work?

An interview of colleagues and friends was next, particularly if Jarrod Whitehouse or Hugh Fraser couldn't be prosecuted.

Gypsy's footsteps rang out on the stairs, and left his work to go into the living room and talk.

She fell onto the couch, out of breath.

He sat beside her. "How did you go?"

"Yeah, okay. I still don't understand why he resists sleep so much. I'd love to be in bed before 8pm."

He shuffled across the couch so that his leg rested against hers. "We need to talk about getting married."

She turned to look at him, her face inches from his. "We don't have the money to get married, we covered this."

"We don't need to have a grand wedding, just you and me at the registry office. Ryan and Christie could be witnesses."

Gypsy smiled at him, rubbing his leg with her left hand. "I like your thinking, but something we need to clear up first."

"I'm listening?"

"This problem you have with what I can do, the psychic stuff. I understand you've accepted your abilities now, but we still need to cover your reasons for insisting I stop that side of things, dampening it down, surely now you see it made no sense?"

"I love you, the family needs you. We almost lost you"

"I know that, I get that, but don't you see? If we're going to get married, we need to move on. That bloke, Reeves, could have killed you. Whether I act on our visions or not, makes no difference. Either one of us could get attacked because of the work we do, psychic or not."

"Yeah, I see that, but what does any of this have to do with getting married?"

"If we're going to be official, I need to be sure you

won't ask me to be something I'm not. You've asked me not to act on my visions and I haven't, but do you think that means miraculously they stopped? I can't shut off that side of my life forever. It's coming between us."

"If we go back to the way we were before the shooting, will you marry me?"

"I thought we covered that. Of course, I'll marry you, but at the right time. Getting married isn't cheap."

"Like I said, we do low key. You, me, a couple of witnesses, and the registry office." He moved closer to her, his lips inches from hers.

"When?"

"Next weekend."

"Next weekend? That's crazy talk. I need a dress, there's stuff to organise."

"You, me, someone to marry us, and that's it. The rest is all a bonus," he said as he leaned across to kiss her. She responded, and he wrapped his arms around her before pulling away. "Let's continue this in our room."

He took her by the hand and led her to their bedroom.

As he undressed for bed, he became aware of streams of energy—powerful energy—beams headed directly for his son. He knew what their intention was: to take over a young body, to inhabit it, a challenge but possible nonetheless. His first instinct was to dart to Mark's room, to stop them in their tracks, but he knew that being physically present would alert whoever was doing this that he was onto them.

He lay down on the bed to tune into his abilities,

concentrating on a fixed point, directly above the ceiling where Mark's bedroom was, through and up into it.

There were three of them in there, playing with Mark, attempting to distract him. It wouldn't work, not if Connor had anything to do with.

He gained access to the connection, emanating from the leader, a cocky and arrogant being, confident in the success of his mission. He'd put out a beam of energy, intense and powerful. Connor scanned it, seeing a visual of multi coloured light, blue and silver, drawing Mark in, attempting to draw him toward the source.

Once Connor locked onto the connection, he snapped it, feeling it with an almost physical force. The being stopped, surprised that it had been intercepted.

Take that, and don't ever, ever mess with my son again.

The being shrank momentarily, and Connor capitalised on the hesitation, pushing the spirit out of the room. The being zoomed away, the less powerful followers right behind it.

Connor scanned the room, ensuring no other spirits had their sights on his son.

He wondered if that would be the end of angry spirits for now or whether Lauren would come back to him and finally reveal her murderer.

\#

CHAPTER 10

The woman's blonde hair hung lank around her distressed face. She stood before him, and the mascara ran down, pooling in the deep depressions of her eyes. She held the tiny baby within the light blue blanket close to her chest.

The wall of blackness behind her gave no indication of her location.

Her mouth opened, calling to Connor but he couldn't hear a word. He strained forward to hear her, gesturing with his right hand for her to speak. He said her name, but she barely reacted.

She continued with her plea, clutching the baby, her cries indecipherable.

"What?" Connor said. "What is it?"

He attempted to say more, but the words remained silent. She held the baby and turned ninety degrees, an attempt to gesture at a point in the distance behind her.

He narrowed his eyes. Lauren was back, not quite so happy this time. She took a step backwards and an object appeared behind her. Dark grey in colour, the thin steel tower almost reached her head. The tears began to flow again and she shook her head, gently sliding her left hand from underneath the bundle. She held onto it tightly, rocking it up and down gently as if to soothe the baby to sleep.

The dark grey object consisted of four square drawers.

A filing cabinet.

He attempted to walk toward it to get a closer look, but his viewpoint didn't change.

"What is it? Tell me, please," he tried to say, but the words remained unspoken. He gave up speaking in that moment, she wasn't interested in what he had to say, he knew in that moment she had an important message to get across to him.

She pointed at the top of the cabinet and her mouth opened fully. Her head moved back as she wailed silently.

On top of the cabinet lay a small object, what appeared to be a tiny black square.

"What is it?" he said again.

She pointed, her mouth a grimace.

He focussed on the object, and it slowly came into focus. A tiny black stamp with a white head on it. A Penny Black.

His stomach rolled and a chill moved up his back. He struggled to breathe.

He opened his eyes and pushed up from the bed to sit up, the fresh gasps of breath coming in huge gulps. The numbers on the alarm clock screamed at him, 7.12am.

He needed to make urgent phone calls. He flung back the bed covers and lurched toward the drawers.

He yanked out his clothes.

When he'd dressed, he reached for his phone charging on the table beside the bed. Gypsy turned in bed, mumbling under her breath. Her alarm would go off soon, anyway.

"Babe.," he called out quietly. Despite the urgency, he didn't want to wake her up suddenly. "Gypsy"

Her eyes opened. "Huh?"

"It's ten past seven, your alarm'll go off soon, anyway. I'm off early."

"How come?"

"Lauren's killer. I've got him."

"Who?"

"I'll call you. I need to confirm with Ryan first."

"Be careful," she said, as she got up out of bed and gave him a sleepy hug.

"Always," he said. kissing the top of her head.

She shuffled away toward the bathroom. He swiped the phone and searched his contacts for the number for Katrina, Elizabeth Metcalfe's only living sister.

It rang six times before it answered.

Her voice was heavy with sleep. "Hello?"

"Katrina, it's Connor Reardon the investigator. Sorry to ring so early but it's urgent. A matter of life and death, in fact."

"What the hell..."

"How's Elizabeth going?"

"Still sedated. With a bit of luck, she slept properly last night."

"What about Leigh? Is he working, or has he taken time off to be with her?"

"Apparently, he got a week's compassionate

leave."

"Are they at home, or the holiday house?"

"The holiday house, why?"

"You're there with them?"

"Yeah, Leigh decided to be a good husband and take Elizabeth to the holiday house. I went with them. Family needs to stick together. I might be her sister in law, but a loss is a loss. Did you skip the sensitivity classes when you got your license? What is this, twenty questions?"

He ignored her comment. "What I'm about to ask you may sound offensive, but please, I need your help. I may have identified the killer."

"Who? I'd love just five minutes with that bastard, I swear..."

"I'll get to that. I need to know, Elizabeth and Leigh, did they have problems in their marriage?"

She blew out a breath. "Listen, I know you said it's important, but can I call you back? It's seven o' clock in the freakin' morning and I'm on leave."

"Did they have problems?"

"Jeez what marriage doesn't? Why do you think I'm still single?"

"I mean fertility problems. They don't have children?"

"Who told you?"

"No one did. I do treat all info I get as confidential. Bear with me, it's a process of elimination. Were they infertile?"

"Yeah. They nearly split up based on what Liz told me. At first, they thought they'd try IVF, then ..."

"Elizabeth had some issues."

Katrina paused. "They talked about adopting. A couple months ago, she said they'd try fostering, so many kids in need and all that. She was trying to get Leigh to come along to the next training session."

"So, it's just the three of you at the holiday house?"

"Yeah. Listen, what's going on?"

"I can't say yet, but please, this is vital, listen carefully. Don't tell anyone I called. Not Elizabeth or Leigh. I should be there by nine o' clock at the latest. Keep it cool and casual. But I need all three of you there this morning. We'll sit down and talk, I promise"

"Why can't you tell me now?"

"Like I said, it's vital. Just between you and me. All three of you need to be there. It's only a couple of hours."

"What do I do if Leigh or Elizabeth want to go out?"

"Just tell them you want to talk. Tell them you've scheduled a meeting with a counsellor or something. Please, I'll be there as soon as I can. I'll leave in the next few minutes if it all comes together."

She hesitated. "Okay, see you soon."

He hung up, almost missing the button as his hands shook. He paused as he headed for the doorway. Backtracking, he moved toward the wooden wardrobe door, opened it and flicked the interior light upward. His gun, long forgotten, hung on its holster at the back. He rifled through the clothing jammed in to near capacity, tugging on the leather strap, and took it in his hands, feeling its weight.

He stood shifting his weight from side to side. His ability to use it under the law was limited as a private investigator, no longer a permanent fixture strapped to his body under his jacket. Reassured by its weight, once his constant companion, he pulled it closer to him.

If he took the weapon the only legal way he could use it would be if the suspect made a run for it, and even then, shooting a suspect in the leg could be questionable, at best.

Yet this worm had remained hidden for too long, assured that the focus would remain on Lauren's husband, Jarrod Whitehouse.

He strapped the holster over his shoulder, the restriction of his torso an almost foreign experience after so long.

The shoulder of the London fog jacket caught his eye. He'd always associated it with being on the beat, yet somehow this case had brought him the closest he'd ever been to being an active sworn member of the force.

He ripped the jacket off the hanger, and slid one arm in and then the other. The long-forgotten kick arse attitude washed over him. He wondered if that was how women felt after putting on make-up, a mask to face the world.

He'd need more than a mask, though, facing a murderer.

He moved through the doorway toward the front door, absorbing the silence of the early hour.

After checking for wallet, keys, and phone, he headed for Black Betty and knew she'd get him there as fast as physically possible. His muscles tensed as he started the car. He hoped traffic wouldn't be too bad and he'd hit the freeway in around ten minutes, all being well. He needed every force known to mankind to go his way right now.

As bright filtered light pierced the windscreen, he pressed the blue tooth button and pushed the down arrow for Ryan's mobile.

After four rings, Ryan answered. "What's up?"

"Look, I know you can't give out information, but I reckon you could give me yes or no answers."

Ryan's voice swung downward. "Yeah...maybe. Ask away, I can't guarantee you'll get an answer."

"Shit, mate, don't go all 'I can't lose my job' on me now. Just yes or no will do."

"No harm in asking."

"Was Lauren pregnant?"

A pause. A few seconds at first, but then it seemed to stretch into oblivion.

At length, Ryan cleared his throat. "Why do you ask?"

"I've been looking in the wrong place, and the worm that did this was pretty damn confident no one would. I need to confirm a suspicion."

"What type of suspicion?"

"A yes or no answer, then I'll answer that. You really want to play this game when the murderer is out there living his middle-class life like nothing ever damn well happened?"

Another pause.

Ryan's voice deepened. "Yes."

"How many weeks? 10? 12? Longer?"

"Yes."

"Yes what?"

Ryan must have the phone close to his face, because the breath shot into the speaker, rippling and rustling and almost bursting Connor's eardrum.

"Don't push it." Said Ryan, biting out the words.

Connor decided to leave that one for now,

choosing to accept a small victory with the first confirmation.

"Can DNA be done on the pregnancy?"

"I guess. I could follow up."

"Do that. Just a hunch. If Whitehouse had a vasectomy, then that DNA could be the key evidence once I arrest this piece of shit." The seed of a thought had sprouted. During her visit, last night, her desperation to hold on to the baby and the emotion she'd pushed into his mind told him, this was a baby she thought she'd never have.

"Arrest? What do you mean arrest?"

"A citizen's arrest. Don't worry, I'm not stupid. I'm hoping he runs. Without that, I can't touch him but once he heads for the hills..."

Connor had reached the freeway. The sun burned orange and white in the sky. The irony of such beauty amongst the activity that was arresting a murderer while the people of Melbourne headed to work wasn't lost on him.

"Okay. So, we've wasted precious hours questioning Tweedle-dee and Tweedledum," Ryan said. "If it isn't Whitehouse or Fraser, who is it?"

"What do you mean wasted? What about fraud? The money was used for blackmail, not renovations. There's fraud and deception right there."

"Whitehouse called in the union rep and dug his heels in. Fraser came close, but without Whitehouse or the Police Prosecutor on board, it's an uphill battle. Apparently, it's closer to a civil case with the bank than anything."

Connor wiped his palm down his pants from thigh to knee. "Second, was there a foreign substance found in the head wound?"

"Foreign substance?"

"I don't see a parrot on my shoulder."

"Funny guy."

"Well, was there? It would be rare, not found commonly, like glue or a trace of something different."

"I'll have to check."

"Do that, urgently. I'm on my way there."

"On your way where?"

"Sorrento, the Metcalfe holiday house."

"The suspect is your client? Or the other sister..."

"No, Einstein, the quiet, unassuming stuffed shirt. The rare stamp collecting brother-in-law hidden off the radar, while you and I run around like chickens with their heads cut off."

"Holy shit."

"Yep. I'm about to make a citizen's arrest."

"Okay. Remember the Crimes Act."

"Mate, I'm not stupid. How could I forget the damn Crimes Act? I worked with it for years. Let's hope he runs."

"If he doesn't…?"

"Then I call it in, anyway."

"I'll look out for it on the D24 dispatch list."

"Right. Talk soon."

"Yeah. You left that dusty old weapon where it belongs, right?"

Connor hung up.

He was about twenty minutes from his ultimate destination, the place where Leigh and Lauren had at first talked about her concerns with not only the finances but her marriage. Leigh had no doubt listened with a serious expression.

Her initial concerns may have become tears, and

the weasel took the opportunity to seduce a lonely, vulnerable mother.

How long did the affair last? Judging by his findings on when the loan was taken out, likely no more than a few months.

A few months to unravel a family, and snuff out a life.

He wondered on how it had all gone down. The spirit of Lauren had directed him to her killer, but not much more than that. He imagined Lauren, approaching her brother in law, distressed and distraught, and he'd advised her, and consoled her. One thing led to another and they'd become intimate. How long had the process taken? He struggled to imagine the conservative worm being lucky enough that Lauren started an affair with him.

Maybe they'd met at the holiday house enough times, and talked through her worries and concerns about her decaying marriage enough that she'd trusted him over time.

Pillow talk might have given the weasel the information he needed, namely that Jarrod Whitehouse had a vasectomy, that he'd been transferred to missing persons, that he was being blackmailed for his secret fetish.

Lauren had probably worked it out, and when she learned of her pregnancy, made plans to leave both her husband and her lover. A gutsy move, but sadly she'd never left.

Connor didn't want to believe she'd leave her daughter behind. They day of her murder she probably left her car at home. The community of Sorrento was small and tight knit and would notice her car parked there at regular intervals.

He imagined her going to Leigh late at night, telling about the pregnancy, and that she didn't intend to keep it. This would've infuriated the worm, his only chance at a biological child.

The worm had pushed her hard against the filing cabinet, where her head hit the corner and she'd fallen unconscious. The worm, assuming he'd killed her, had then driven out to a quiet spot and buried her in the shallow grave, not knowing she'd been alive, and would never regain consciousness.

With little to give his thoughts away, barely a flicker of the muscles around his jaw, Connor turned off the freeway and onto a main road, Cassowary Road.

The indicator flicked on and off, a quiet ticking, a time bomb with outcome unknown.

The holiday house lay in a maze of quiet courts and back streets, a nest of peaceful family holidays, relaxation, and fun for many of them. Not this family.

He wondered if the worm had any idea, any inclination, that his deadly act had been uncovered, or considered the possibility for even a moment.

A slight bump vibrated beneath him as the road switched from bitumen to gravel narrowing to a single lane due to low traffic.

They'd see him coming. Although he wasn't sure why that worried him, Black Betty's growling could be heard from streets away.

As gravel crunched below the slow moving tyres, the hairs on the back of his neck prickled up. The sensation that someone sat in the back seat washed over him. He stopped the car, twisting his neck to look at the back seat.

He saw her, leaning back quite relaxed, but this

time not wailing or crying, rather a smile of contentment. She held the baby closer to her chest, watching the baby. Lauren barely moved other than to pat its bottom.

No pressure or anything.

He pulled into the driveway, parking behind the silver car, effectively barring escape.

If the worm ran, he'd need to run on foot. It had been a long time since Connor had conducted a car chase.

The home appeared unchanged, stuck in a time warp from the seventies, not unlike its owner.

He knocked on the door, and the sound echoed throughout the small hallway into the lounge room beyond.

Within seconds, Katrina opened the door, the bags under her eyes pronounced. Her face appeared hollowed out.

"You're here, thank god." Katrina said.

He took a step onto the carpet, ignoring the garish multi-colored swirls in regular intervals across it. He stared instead at Leigh Metcalfe, bent over a travel bag in front of the couch which had been pushed against the wall.

Connor tried to appear nonchalant. "Going somewhere?"

Leigh paused, and then straightened his spine, mouth open and eyes wide. "Oh, er, not really, but now that Katrina's here, it's time to get back to reality. The week's leave's nearly over."

The worm thought he could carry on like nothing had ever happened. Connor's fingers curled into his palms so hard his nails were leaving an imprint. He wanted to punch the bastard, and hard, but the last thing he needed was another possible assault case. This would be a clean arrest, by the book.

"What about your wife?" Connor made no move from the doorway.

Reardon took a small step closer toward Leigh. Of course, despite being on leave, the stuffed shirt still wore business clothes, dark suit paints, blue shirt, his sole concession to the situation, the absence of a necktie.

"She's sleeping most of the time. Not a great deal I can do."

"No, I suppose not, especially when you're the reason she's suffering."

"I resent that remark--" Leigh rubbed the side of his nose then stared at the floor.

Katrina strode across to stand at Connor's left side, in between them.

"I told him a counsellor was on the way. He told me we didn't need one and to cancel it. He wouldn't leave me alone, badgered me constantly until I caved and told him you were on the way." She blew a hair out of her mouth. "I'm sorry."

"I'm here now, that's all that matters."

Run, you bastard, please run.

The worm pushed up his glasses, posture bent. Since the last time Connor had seen him, Leigh Metcalfe appeared to have aged significantly and the dark circles under his eyes stood out like bleak hollowed beacons in his pasty white face.

Connor's phone buzzed in his pocket and rang, quietly at first, then louder with each passing second. He took it out and brought it to his ear, keeping his stare fixed on Leigh. Katrina hovered a foot or so away, refusing to make eye contact and biting her lip.

"Ryan. Just arrived."

"Okay," Ryan said, dragging the word out to elongate it.

"Tell me you're calling with an answer to my question about the head wound?"

Leigh Metcalfe leaned away from him.

"Yeah. I checked. They weren't too happy about being pushed to get results quickly, but I have it. A glue-like substance, not seen often, pretty old, from say the nineteen hundreds found in the wound."

"From a rare stamp?"

"Something like that." Ryan's voice quietened to a rumble.

"Thanks. Can you ask for DNA tests on the foetus?"

Katrina's head snapped up, her eyes suddenly rivetted on the mobile telephone.

"Yeah, I'll let you know," Ryan said. "Take care."

"Right. Call you back...later."

Connor folded the phone back into his pocket and looked at Katrina, and then Leigh.

Katrina took a step forward, her shoulders high and tight, and extended her hand with palms up. "What the hell was that about?"

"The Coroner's findings."

"You mentioned a pregnancy?" Katrina said, voice shrill.

Leigh had turned away and paced in a small circle, hands on hips.

"Lauren was pregnant. You knew that, though, didn't you, Leigh? She told you. As the father, you had the right to know."

Katrina's eyes widened at Leigh. "What the hell?"

Leigh threw down the shirt he was packing into his

luggage. He spun around, pointing at Connor. "How dare you! What would you know? This is none of your business. We're still grieving. Leave us in peace! Get out, now!"

Despite his heart thudding in his chest, Connor stayed cool, conscious of keeping his voice quiet and measured.

He did his best not to hiss through gritted teeth. "I know Lauren was pregnant, which is pretty difficult given her husband had a vasectomy. Know anything about that?"

Leigh looked down, using his hair as a shield. He zipped the bag and then picked up the handle. "If you'll excuse me, I need to get to work."

"I don't think so," Connor said, barring the doorway. He slid his right arm under his jacket, feeling the smoothness of the gun handle. "It's easy enough to confirm the father of the foetus. DNA can do amazing things these days."

Katrina surged forward, bent at the waist, pointing her finger in her brother-in-law's face. "You bastard. You were having an affair with Lauren, of all the low life, conniving scum—"

Leigh cut her off, palm facing her face. "Don't believe it for a second. He's fishing, seeing if his theory fits, and it doesn't, not for a minute."

"If it's a theory, I'm sure you won't mind giving a DNA sample to eliminate you from the investigation," Connor said, and then paused.

Both he and Katrina glared at Leigh, a sheen of sweat shining on his face. He made no move to wipe it away.

"It doesn't prove anything," Leigh said at last.

"It proves you're the father, and you had motive.

She called it off, didn't she? One last meeting. She told you she'd terminated the pregnancy, which infuriated you, your only chance at having a biological child. Except she lied, maybe she intended to leave her husband, but she certainly didn't want a future with you anymore."

Leigh lunged toward Connor, hands out toward his throat. Connor grabbed his outstretched hands. He twisted Leigh around, wrapping both his own hands around Leigh's windpipe.

"You bastard," Connor hissed in the worm's ear. "You killed her. You can tell yourself it was an accident all you want but you pushed her so hard her head hit the cabinet. That's how the glue got into the head wound. You kept your stamps there, the Penny Black."

"I. Can't. Breathe," Leigh whispered.

For a moment, Connor considered pulling to tighten the grip, then released him. Leigh rubbed his throat. "You're a savage, pure and simple."

"Maybe, but I didn't kill a pregnant woman."

"It was an accident. I didn't mean to hurt her..." Leigh's face changed from pale to almost purple, and he balled his hands into fists.

Katrina rushed forward, hitting him in the chest.

"You killed my sister! You piece of shit we trusted you, Liz trusted you, you bastard!" Her words spun out of control, becoming almost indecipherable at such skyrocketing pitch.

Connor extricated her from Leigh, as gently as possible. "He's not worth it."

Her words cracked into tears, and she collapsed against the couch, covering her face in her hands.

"He'll get his punishment," Connor murmured

quietly.

Leigh rubbed his red throat. "I'll charge you with assault."

"Self-defense," Connor said, the muscles in his cheek twitching as he fought to control his anger. "I'm sure you'll say the same when you're charged. Good luck defending the indefensible. Lauren was alive when you buried her. She suffocated to death. You murdered her, pure and simple." He bit the words out, solid and heavy.

Leigh Metcalfe stood glaring at Connor, pushing air out through his teeth. A purple vein engorged in his temple. Time seemed to slow down. Leigh's eyes glassed over, then he fell, knees buckling, and landed backwards, his head barely missing the couch as he hit the carpet with a loud thump.

Connor stared at the still form on the carpet. He took a moment to get his breath, removed his phone from his pocket and dialled triple zero.

"Hello? I'd like to report a murder suspect here in Sorrento." He paused. "I've made a citizen's arrest, and the suspect collapsed in the living room."

Connor gave them the address details to make an arrest, before sitting on the couch. Across the room, Katrina stared at the wall unseeing, almost catatonic, probably in shock. Finding out her brother in law was a murdered in was rough for anyone to take in, especially the way this had unfolded.

Leigh had rested back cocky and smug, sure that due to information Elizabeth provided, all investigations would point to Jarred Whitehouse. His murdered mistress had made sure Connor looked in the right place. At that moment, despite his bones aching and feeling every ounce of energy leave, he saw her transparent figure, walking in from the hallway. She floated toward Katrina on the couch, wrapping her arms around her shoulders, moving her cheek next to hers, and touching it gently.

Connor wasn't sure whether to tell Katrina. Considering what she had been through, he decided to keep quiet. She didn't need anything else to stir her emotions further.

Wiping tears from under her eyes, she turned to face him, hunched forward at the other end of the couch. "I don't believe this. After all the crap we've been through, all the torment, suddenly, I feel peaceful, like everything will turn out all right. Maybe Lauren's watching, pleased that we caught the bastard that did this to her."

Connor nodded, rubbing at his chin. "Maybe she is, Katrina. Maybe she is."

###

EPILOGUE

The woman's blonde hair hung lank around her distressed face. She stood before him, and the mascara ran down, pooling in the deep depressions of her eyes. She held the tiny baby within the light blue blanket close to her chest.

Inky darkness had replaced the twilight when Connor left the local police station out on the Peninsula. He'd watched the sky's progression during the interview with police, and as he detailed the various twists and turn of events, the view through the window had turned from glaring piercing light, to faded brightness, and dull pre-sunset, the curtain of night falling as he told of Elizabeth's visit, followed by his interviews with Jarrod Whitehouse, and later Hugh Fraser.

Of course, he'd conveniently omitted any references to his Sentinel abilities, explaining away the final clue through serendipity, that somehow it had taken time for the pieces to fall into place and for the puzzle to be solved, which wasn't strictly a lie. Quite often investigations took time, for the seemingly random factors to come together, usually when least expected.

Ryan had arrived toward the end of the interview, and of course, he hadn't mentioned that had it not been for Ryan providing information to him, the investigation would most likely have taken a lot longer.

After the interview, they stood on the top step, looking out at the view: tall trees nodding in agreement, as the wind shifted through the leaves. A couple of holiday makers remained, sitting on a blanket, laughing as they enjoyed the remnants of the day.

Seagulls called out to them, and the peace and tranquility of the area flowed through him. The investigation had ended.

"Might check on my client tomorrow," Connor said as he bowed his head and trudged down the steps. "She's had a lot to deal with."

"Yeah," Ryan said, shoving his hands in his pockets. "It's not every day you lose a sister and a husband in one move."

Connor reached the bottom of the steps and paused on the footpath. "I'm thinking of putting in an application, a return to Homicide."

Ryan arched one eyebrow. "You are? I wasn't expecting that."

"I don't know." He sighed. "Private Investigation has been good to me for a while, but since I lost the contract, I don't know, something's changed."

"Yeah, mate." Ryan removed his hands from his pockets. "They could use you in Homicide. Or in the Academy. There's an instructor job going, a couple of days a week."

"I'll think about it," Connor said, and he turned the corner toward the car park. Ryan followed behind him.

New native bushes and grasses had been planted, and the markings of a fresh watering left fan shapes on the concrete. Connor reached his car and opened the door. "Any charges for Whitehouse or Fraser?"

"Barely," Ryan said, heading a few feet away to his own vehicle. "Police prosecutor didn't go for it. Blackmail charges for Fraser most likely. Fraud might become a civil case if the bank ever gets through the red tape."

Connor didn't bother replying.

"Anyway, I'm heading home." He realised he was about to tell Ryan about his plans to get married in the next couple of weeks, and then paused. "Hey Ryan, I wanted to ask you something."

Ryan gazed at a uniformed officer walking away from a car, watching as the figure became smaller. Then they were alone again.

After a moment, he walked toward Connor and stood directly in front of him. "What is it?"

Connor rubbed at his chin. There didn't seem to be an easy way to say it. He didn't fancy the idea of a sentimental moment in the back of a police station in the outer suburbs of the Mornington Peninsula, but he'd started. "I was talking to Gypsy, about getting married. She said she wants to wait until we have the money. Something is holding her back, I can sense it, and I don't think it's me, or at least, I hope not."

Ryan smiled, shoving his hands in his pockets. He shifted his weight to his right hip, waiting for a response.

Somehow, getting to the point seemed difficult, needing the perfect segue which proved out of reach. What the hell, better to just come right out with it.

"When she gets over her idea that getting married will make a respectable woman out of her, I'll need a best man, and I can't think of a better man than you."

Ryan's mouth dropped open, but he quickly closed it, before his lips formed a grin. "I'd be honoured, mate." He flushed. "I'm not sure what else to say, but...thanks, I guess."

"No problem," Connor said, looking down at the

concrete. He'd never been good with sentimentality, particularly raw unbridled emotions like whatever the hell it was that surged in his chest. "I'll head off, but..."

What did he want to say? Somehow, thanks for risking your career to give me the answers I needed to solve the case didn't cover it. Besides, he'd never say that sort of stuff, anyway. It smacked of desperation.

Instead, he grinned at Ryan.

With a chuckle, Ryan waved and headed back to his car. Connor watched as Ryan backed out and disappeared down the street. He hesitated, taking in another glance of the sky, and then headed home. He couldn't wait to tell Gypsy this case was over.

- End -

Also by Andrea **Drew**

The Gypsy Medium Series:

Book 1 – Gypsy Hunted

Book 2 –Gypsy Cradle

Book 3 –Gypsy Curse

193

The adventure continues . . .

Follow the adventures of Connor Reardon and Gypsy Shields here at: www.andreadrewauthor.com

Stay in touch with the author via:
https://www.amazon.com/Andrea-Drew/e/B009KC2QXS

Facebook:
https://www.facebook.com/authorandreadrew/

Twitter: http://twitter.com/drewwriter

If you liked Sentinel Rising, please post a review at Amazon, and let your friends know about the Reardon Files and the Gypsy Medium Series.